V 9c

Welcome to the world
of Sydney Harbour Hospital

(or *SHH…* for short—
because secrets never stay hidden for long!)

Looking out over cosmopolitan Sydney Harbour, Australia's premier teaching hospital is a hive of round-the-clock activity—with a *very* active hospital grapevine.

With the most renowned (and gorgeous!) doctors in Sydney working side by side, professional and sensual tensions run sky-high—there's *always* plenty of romantic rumours to gossip about…

Who's been kissing who in the on-call room? What's going on between legendary heart surgeon Finn Kennedy and tough-talking A&E doctor Evie Lockheart? And what's wrong with Finn?

Find out in this enthralling new eight-book continuity from Medical Romance™—indulge yourself with eight helpings of romance, emotion and gripping medical drama!

Sydney Harbour Hospital
From saving lives to sizzling seduction, these doctors are the very best!

Dear Reader

When I was asked to be part of the *Sydney Harbour Hospital* continuity series I was extremely excited and jumped right in. I was so keen to be joining a group of fellow Australian writers and friends in a mission to bring eight exciting, heart-warming, pulse-thumping and utterly romantic stories to our readers.

Lexi's an energetic whirlwind, super-organised and yet impetuous. She's the type who click-clacks in on her sky-high heels where angels fear to tiptoe in their bedsocks! She dives into things and gets things done—one way or the other.

Sam, on the other hand, is quiet, measured and takes only calculated risks. He never rushes in and is cool, controlled and clinical under pressure...*except* when he's around gorgeous Lexi Lockheart! Then his control slips alarmingly!

Sam and Lexi's brief whirlwind affair five years ago almost derailed Sam's career, and he left the country in order to salvage it. But, unbeknownst to Sam, Lexi suffered terrible heartbreak over the way their affair ended, although she hides all that behind her sassy socialite façade.

Sam's return to SHH just weeks before Lexi is about to marry one of the hospital's biggest supporters is not the only fly in the ointment, however. The attraction Sam and Lexi still feel for each other has implications not just for them, but for others as well.

I really loved writing this story. Sam and Lexi seemed very real to me, and most of the time I felt as if I was just documenting what was going on. I felt like one of those court transcript typists, madly trying to keep up!

I hope you enjoy their lively banter and get totally swept away by how they fall in love—this time for ever.

Warmest wishes

Melanie Milburne

SYDNEY HARBOUR HOSPITAL: HOSPITAL: LEXI'S SECRET

BY
MELANIE MILBURNE

*To Ricki Peres for her friendship and support,
and also for her help in the research for this novel
in the field of transplant surgery. Thank you!*

First published in Great Britain 2012
by Mills & Boon, an imprint of Harlequin (UK) Limited.
Large Print edition 2012
Harlequin (UK) Limited, Eton House,
18-24 Paradise Road, Richmond, Surrey TW9 1SR

© Harlequin Books S.A. 2012

Special thanks and acknowledgement are given
to Melanie Milburne for her contribution to the
Sydney Harbour Hospital series

ISBN: 978 0 263 22482 5

Harlequin (UK) policy is to use papers that are natural, renewable and recyclable products and made from wood grown in sustainable forests. The logging and manufacturing process conform to the legal environmental regulations of the country of origin.

Printed and bound in Great Britain
by CPI Antony Rowe, Chippenham, Wiltshire

From as soon as **Melanie Milburne** could pick up a pen she knew she wanted to write. It was when she picked up her first Harlequin Mills and Boon® at seventeen that she realised she wanted to write romance. Distracted for a few years by meeting and marrying her own handsome hero, surgeon husband Steve, and having two boys, plus completing a Masters of Education and becoming a nationally ranked athlete (Masters swimming) she decided to write. Five submissions later she sold her first book, and is now a multi-published, award-winning, *USA TODAY* bestselling author. In 2008 she won the Australian Readers' Association most popular category/series romance, and in 2011 she won the prestigious Romance Writers of Australia R*BY award.

Melanie loves to hear from her readers via her website: www.melaniemilburne.com.au or on Facebook www.facebook.com/pages/Melanie-Milburne/351594482609

Recent titles by the same author:

THE SURGEON SHE NEVER FORGOT
THE MAN WITH THE LOCKED AWAY HEART

**Praise for Melanie Milburne
who also writes for
Mills & Boon® Modern™ Romance:**

'Expertly blending powerful emotions
with red-hot sensuality, poignant romance
and nail-biting drama, HIS POOR LITTLE RICH GIRL
is an exceptional tale of lost love, courage and redemption
from one of the most accomplished writers
of Mills & Boon® Modern™ Romance!'

Melanie Milburne's
SURRENDERING ALL BUT HER HEART
is also out this month in
Mills & Boon Modern™ Romance!

**These books are also available in eBook format
from www.millsandboon.co.uk**

Sydney Harbour Hospital

Sexy surgeons, dedicated doctors,
scandalous secrets, on-call dramas…

Welcome to the world of Sydney Harbour Hospital
(or *SHH…* for short—
because secrets never stay hidden for long!)

New nurse Lily got caught up in the hotbed of hospital gossip in
SYDNEY HARBOUR HOSPITAL: LILY'S SCANDAL
by Marion Lennox

And gorgeous paediatrician Teo came to single mum Zoe's rescue in
SYDNEY HARBOUR HOSPITAL: ZOE'S BABY
by Alison Roberts

Then sexy Sicilian playboy Luca finally met his match in
SYDNEY HARBOUR HOSPITAL: LUCA'S BAD GIRL
by Amy Andrews

And Hayley opened Tom's eyes to love in
SYDNEY HARBOUR HOSPITAL: TOM'S REDEMPTION
by Fiona Lowe

This month heiress Lexi learns to put the past behind her…
SYDNEY HARBOUR HOSPITAL: LEXI'S SECRET
by Melanie Milburne

There are three more books to come in this fantastic series

SYDNEY HARBOUR HOSPITAL: BELLA'S WISHLIST
by Emily Forbes

SYDNEY HARBOUR HOSPITAL: MARCO'S TEMPTATION
by Fiona McArthur

SYDNEY HARBOUR HOSPITAL: AVA'S RE-AWAKENING
by Carol Marinelli

And not forgetting *Sydney Harbour Hospital's* legendary heart
surgeon Finn Kennedy. This brooding maverick keeps his women
on hospital rotation… But can new doc Evie Lockheart unlock the
secrets to his guarded heart? Find out in this enthralling new eight-
book continuity from Mills & Boon® Medical Romance™.

A collection impossible to resist!

These books are also available in ebook format
from www.millsandboon.co.uk

CHAPTER ONE

IT WAS the worst possible way to run into an ex, Lexi thought. There was only one parking space left in the Sydney Harbour Hospital basement car park and although, strictly speaking, she shouldn't have been parking there since she wasn't a doctor or even a nurse, she was running late with some things for her sister, and it was just too tempting not to grab the last 'Doctors Only' space between a luxury sedan and a shiny red sports car that looked as if it had just been driven out of the showroom.

She opened her door and winced when she heard the bang-scrape of metal against metal.

And then she saw him.

He was sitting in the driver's seat, his broad-spanned hands gripping the steering-wheel with white-knuckled force, glaring at her furiously when recognition suddenly hit him. Lexi saw the quick spasm of his features, as if the sight of her had been like a punch to the face.

She felt the same punch deep and low in her belly as she encountered that dark brown espresso coffee gaze. Her throat closed over as if a large hand had gripped her and was squeezing the breath right out of her. Her heart pounded with a sickening thud, skip, thud, skip, thud that made her feel as if she had just run up the fire escape of a towering skyscraper on a single breath.

It was so unexpected.

No warning.

No preparation.

Why hadn't she been told he was back in the country? Why hadn't she been told he was working *here*? He clearly was, otherwise why would he be parking in the doctors' car park unless— like her—he had flouted the rules for his own convenience?

OK, so this was the time to play it cool. She could do that. It was her specialty. She was known all over the Sydney social circuit for her PhD in charm.

She shimmied out of the tight space between

their cars and sent him a megawatt smile. 'Hi, Sam,' she said breezily. 'How are things?'

Sam Bailey unfolded his tall length from the sports car, closing the driver's door with a re-sounding click that more or less summed up his personality, Lexi thought—decisive, to the point, focussed on the task at hand.

'Alexis,' he said. No "How are you?" or "Nice to see you" or even "Hello", just her full name, which nobody ever called her, not even her father in one of his raging rants or her mother in one of her gin-soaked ramblings.

Lexi's winning smile faded slightly and her hands fidgeted with the strap of her designer bag hanging over her shoulder as she stood before him. 'So, what brings you here?' she said. 'A patient perhaps?'

'You could say that,' he said coolly. 'How about you?'

'Oh, I hang out here a lot,' she said, shifting her weight from one high heel to the other. 'My sister Bella's in and out for treatment all the time. She's been in for the last couple of weeks. Another chest infection. She's on the transplant list but we have to wait until it clears. The chest infection, I mean.' Lexi knew she was rambling but what else could she do? Five years ago she had thought they'd had a future together. Their connection had been sudden but intense. She had dreamed of sharing her life with him and yet without notice Sam had cut her out of his life coldly and ruthlessly, not even pausing long enough to say goodbye. Seeing him again with no notice, no time to prepare herself, had stirred up deeply buried emotions so far beneath the surface she had almost forgotten they were there.

Almost…

'Sorry to hear that,' Sam said making a point of glancing at his silver watch.

Lexi felt a sinkhole of sadness open up inside her. He couldn't have made it clearer he wanted nothing to do with her. How could he be so… so distant after the intense intimacy they had shared? Had their affair meant nothing to him? Nothing at all? Surely she was worth a few minutes of his precious time in spite of the different paths their lives had taken? 'I didn't know you were back from wherever you went,' she said. 'I heard you got a scholarship to study overseas. Where did you go?'

'America,' he said flatly.

She raised her eyebrows, determined to counter his taciturn manner with garrulous charm. 'Wow, that's impressive,' she said. 'The States is so cool. So much to see. So much to do. You must've been the envy of all the other trainees, getting that chance to train abroad.'

'Yes.' Another frowning glance at his watch.

Lexi's gaze went to the strongly boned, deeply tanned wrist he had briefly exposed from the crisp, light blue business shirt he was wearing. Her stomach shifted like a pair of crutches slipping on a sheet of cracked ice. Those wrists had once held her much smaller ones in a passionate exchange that had left her body tingling for hours afterwards. Every moment of their blistering two-week affair was imprinted on her flesh. Seeing him again awakened every sleeping cell of her body to zinging, pulsing life. It felt like her blood had been thawed from a five-year deep freeze. It was racing through the network of her veins like a flash flood, making her heart hammer with the effort.

Her gaze slipped to his mouth, that beautiful sculpted mouth that had moved against hers with such heart-stopping skill. She still remembered the taste of him: minty and fresh and something essentially, potently male. She still remembered the feel of his tongue stroking against hers, the sexy rasp of it as it cajoled hers into a sizzling hot tango. He had explored every inch of her mouth with masterful expertise, leaving no corner without the branding heat of his possession.

And yet he had still walked away without so much as a word.

Lexi lifted her gaze back to his. Encountering those unfathomable brown depths made her chest feel like a frightened bird was trapped inside the cage of her lungs. Did he have any idea of the hurt he had caused? Did he have any idea of what she had gone through because of him?

She swallowed in anguish as she thought of the heart-wrenching decision she had made. Would she ever be able to summon up the courage to tell him? But, then, what would be the point? How could he possibly understand how hard it had been for her back then, young and pregnant with no one to turn to? She hadn't felt ready to become a mother. A termination had seemed the right thing to do and yet…

'I have to get going,' Sam said, nodding towards the hospital building. 'The CEO is expecting me.'

Lexi stared at him as realisation slowly dawned. 'You're going to be working here?' she asked.

'Yes.'

'Here at SHH?'

'Yes.'

'Not in the private sector?' she asked.

'No.'

'Do you ever answer a question with more than one word?'

'Occasionally.'

Lexi gave him a droll look but inside she was screaming: *This can't be happening!* 'Why wasn't I told?' she asked.

'No idea.'

'Wow, that's two.'

'Two what?' he said, frowning.

'Words,' she said. 'Maybe we can work on that a little. Boost your repertoire a bit. What are you doing here?'

'Working.'

She mentally rolled her eyes. 'I mean why here? Why not in the private system where you can earn loads and loads of money?' *Why not some other place where I won't see you just about every day and be reminded of what a silly little fool I was?*

'I was asked.'

'Wow, three words,' Lexi said, purposely animating her expression. 'We're really doing great here. I bet I can get you to say a full sentence in a month or two.'

'I have to go now,' he said. 'And, yes, that's five words if you're still counting.'

She lifted her chin. 'I am.'

Sam looked into those bluer than blue eyes and felt as if he had just dived into the deepest, most refreshing ocean after walking through the driest, hottest desert for years. Her softly pouting mouth was one of those mouths that just begged to be kissed. He could recall the dewy soft contours under his own just by looking at her. He could even remember the feel of the sexy dart of her tongue as it played catch-me-if-you-can with his. Her platinum-blonde hair was in its usual disarray that somehow managed to look perfectly coiffed and just-out-of-bed-after-marathon-sex at the same time. He felt the rocket blast to his groin as he remembered having her in his bed, up against the wall, over his desk, on a picnic blanket under the stars…

Stop it, buddy, he remonstrated with himself.

She had been too young for him before, and in spite of the years a world of experience separated them now. She was still a spoilt, rich kid who thought partying was a full-time occupation. He was on a mission to save lives that were dependent on transplant surgery.

Other people had to die in order for him to give life to others. He was *always* aware of that. Someone lost their life and by doing so he was given the opportunity to save another. He didn't take his responsibility lightly. He had worked long and hard for his career. It had defined his life. He had given up everything to get where he was now. He could not afford, at this crucial time in his journey, to be distracted by a party girl whose biggest decision in life was whether to have floating candles or helium balloons at a function.

He had to walk away, just as he had before,

but at least this would be his choice, made of his own free will.

'You dented my car.' It was not the best line he could have come up with but he had just taken delivery of the damned vehicle. To him it just showed how irresponsible she was. She hadn't even looked as she'd flung open her door. It was just so typical of her and her privileged background. She had no idea how hard people had to work to get things she took for granted. She had been driven around in luxury cars all of her life. She didn't know what it felt like to be dirt poor with no funds available for extras, let alone the essentials.

Just take his mother, for instance. Stuck on a long transplant list and living way out in the bush to boot, his mother had died waiting for a kidney. His working-class parents hadn't had the money to pay for private health cover. They hadn't even had the money to afford another child after him. He knew what it felt like to want things that were so out of your reach it was like grasping at bubbles, hoping they wouldn't burst when your fingers touched them. In his experience they always burst.

Lexi was another bubble that had burst.

'You call that a dent?' Lexi bent over to examine the mark on the door.

Sam couldn't stop his gaze drinking in the gorgeous curve of her tiny bottom. She was all legs and arms, coltish, even though she was now twenty-four. It didn't seem to matter what she wore, she always looked like she had just stepped off a catwalk. Her legs were encased in skin-tight black pants that followed the long lines of her legs down to her racehorse-delicate ankles. She was wearing ridiculously high heels but he still had a few inches on her. The hot-pink top she had on skimmed her small but perfectly shaped breasts and the ruby-and-diamond pendant she was wearing around her neck looked like it could have paid off his entire university tuition loan.

She smelled fabulous. He felt his nostrils flaring to breathe more of her fragrance in. Flowers, spring flowers with a grace note of sexy sandalwood, or was it patchouli?

She suddenly straightened and met his eyes. 'It's barely made a mark,' she said. 'But if you want to be so pedantic I'll pay for it to be fixed.'

Sam elevated one of his brows mockingly. 'Don't you mean Daddy will pay for it?' he asked.

She pursed her mouth at him and he had to stop himself from bending down and covering it with his own. 'I'll have you know I earn my own money,' she said with a haughty look.

'Doing what?' he shot back. 'Painting your nails?'

She narrowed her blue eyes and her full mouth flattened. 'I'm Head of Events at SHH,' she said. 'I'm in charge of fundraising, including the gala masked ball to be held next month.'

Sam rocked back on his heels. 'Impressive.'

She gave him a hot little glare. 'My father gave me the job because I'm good at what I do.'

'I'm sure you are,' he said. *After all, partying was her favourite hobby.* 'Now, if you'll excuse me, I have a meeting to get to.'

'Is this your first day at SHH?' Lexi asked.

'Yes.'

'Where are you living?'

'I'm renting an apartment in Kirribilli,' he said. 'I want to have a look around before I buy.'

A small frown puckered her smooth brow. 'So you're back for good?' she asked.

'Yes,' Sam said. 'My father's getting on and I want to spend some time with him.'

'Is he still living in Broken Hill?' she asked.

'No,' he said. 'He's retired to the Central Coast.'

Sam was surprised she remembered anything about his father. It didn't sit well with his image of her as a shallow, spoilt little upstart who had only jumped into bed with him as an act of rebellion against her overbearing father.

That had really rankled.

Damn it, it *still* rankled.

Their red-hot affair had only lasted a couple of weeks before her father Richard Lockheart had stepped in and told him what would happen to his career if he didn't stop messing with his baby girl. To top it all off, it turned out she was six years younger than she had told him. It had been a jolting shock to find the young woman he had been sleeping with had only left high school the year before. Nineteen years old and yet she had looked and acted as streetwise and poised as any twenty-five-year-old.

Sam had told her things during that short affair he had told no one else. Things about his mother's death, like how hard it had been to watch her die, feeling so helpless, his father's endless grieving, his own dreams of making a difference so no one had to go through what his family had suffered. For once in his life his emotional guard had come down and it had backfired on him. Lexi had used him like she used her social standing to get what she wanted. He had almost lost everything because of her puerile, attention-seeking little game.

When it came down to it, it had been a choice between relocating or sitting back and watching his career implode. To a working-class trainee who had lived on Struggle Street for most of his life, Sam knew that the well-connected and powerful Richard Lockheart could have done some serious damage to his career. He hadn't taken those threats lightly. He had been lucky enough to be able to switch to the US training programme, and while it had cost him a packet, it had been the best thing he'd ever done. He had worked with some of the world's leading trans-plant surgeons and now he was considered one of the best heart-lung surgeons on the planet. Everyone back home had believed he had transferred on a scholarship and he hadn't said anything to contradict the rumour. Interestingly, neither, it seemed, had Richard Lockheart.

The appointment to SHH had been timely because he had been keen to come home for a couple of years. He missed his homeland and his father. The man was the only family he had. It was time to come home and put the past behind him.

Lexi was a part of his past but she had no place in his future. He had been captivated by her beauty and her alluring sensuality. But her party-girl mentality had been at odds with his career-focussed determination back then—just as much as it was at odds with it now. He couldn't afford to be distracted by her. Even though the eleven-year age gap was no longer such an issue he didn't want anything or anyone—particularly not red-hot little Lexi Lockheart—derailing his career plans.

Lexi flicked a strand of hair away that had drifted across her face. 'How will I contact you?' she asked.

Sam's brows snapped together. 'About what?'

'About your car,' she said, with another little mocking quiver of her eyelids. 'About the dent you need a magnifying glass to see.'

'Forget about it,' he said.

'No, I insist,' she said, taking out her mobile. 'I'll put you in my contacts.' Her slim, beautifully manicured fingers poised over the data entry key.

And that's when he saw it.

The diamond engagement ring on her finger seemed to be glinting at him like an evil eye, mocking him, taunting him.

Engaged.

He felt his throat seize up.

Lexi was engaged.

His mouth was suddenly so dry he couldn't speak. His chest felt as if someone had backed over it with a steamroller. He couldn't inflate his lungs enough to draw in a breath. His reaction surprised him. No, damn it, it shocked the hell out of him. She was nothing to him. What did it matter if she was engaged? It wasn't as if he had any claim on her, certainly not an emotional one. He didn't do emotion. He didn't even like her, for goodness' sake. She was an attention-seeking little tramp who thought bedding a boy from the bush was something to giggle about with her vacuous, equally shallow socialite girl-friends. Good luck to the man who was fool enough to tie himself to her.

Lexi looked up at him with an expectant expression. 'Your number?' she prompted.

Sam reluctantly rattled it off in a monotone he hardly recognised as his own voice. He had changed his number five years ago as a way of completely cutting all ties. He hadn't wanted her calling him or texting him or emailing him. He didn't want that soft sexy voice purring in his ear. It had taken years to get the sound of her voice out of his head.

Engaged.

Sam wondered what her fiancé was like. No, on second thought he didn't want to know. He'd bet he was a preppy sort, probably hadn't done a decent day's work in his life.

Lexi was engaged. Engaged!

It was a two-sentence chant he couldn't get out of his head. Cruel words he didn't want to hear.

'Do you want mine?' she asked, tucking another wayward strand of platinum-blonde hair away from her face with her free hand. It had snagged on her shiny lip gloss. He guessed it was strawberry flavoured. He hadn't eaten a strawberry in five years without thinking of the taste of her mouth.

He blinked. 'Your...er what?'

'My number,' she said. 'In case you want to contact me about the repairs?'

Sam swallowed the walnut-sized restriction in his throat. 'Your car isn't damaged.'

She looked at him for a moment before she closed her phone and popped it back in her bag. 'No,' she said. 'It's made of much tougher stuff, apparently.'

Sam's gaze kept tracking to her ring. It was like a magnet he had no power to resist. He didn't want to look at it. He didn't want to think about her planning a future with some other nameless, faceless man.

He didn't want to think about her in that nameless, faceless man's bed, her arms around his neck and her lips on his.

'You're engaged.'

He hadn't realised he had spoken the words out loud until she answered, 'Yes.'

'Congratulations,' he said.

'Thank you.'

Sam's gaze tracked back to the ring. It was expensive. It suited her hand. It was a perfect fit. It looked like it had been there a while.

His chest cramped again, harder this time.

He brought his eyes back to hers, forcing his voice to sound just mildly interested. 'So, when's the wedding?'

'November,' she said, a flicker of something moving over her face like a shadow. 'We've booked the cathedral for the tenth.'

The silence crawled from the dark corners of the basement, slowly but surely surrounding them.

Sam heard the scrape of one of her heels as she took a step backwards. 'Well, I'd better let you get to work,' she said. 'Wouldn't be good to be late for your first day on the job.'

'No,' he said. 'That might not go down so well.'

The silence crept up to his knees again before he added, 'It was nice to see you again, Alexis.'

She gave a tight smile by way of answer and

walked off towards the lift, the sound of her heels click-clacking on the concrete floor striking totally unexpected and equally inexplicable hammer blows of regret in Sam's heart.

CHAPTER TWO

LEXI got out on the medical ward floor with her heart still racing. She had to control her spiralling emotions, but how? How was she supposed to act as if nothing was wrong?

Sam was back.

The shock was still reverberating through her like a dinner gong struck too hard. Her head was aching from the tattoo beating inside her brain.

Sam was back.

She drew in a calming breath. She would have to act as if nothing was wrong. It wouldn't do to reveal to everyone how shocked she was by his appointment. Had no one told her because they were worried how she would react or because they thought she wouldn't even remember him? And how could she ask without drawing attention to feelings she didn't want—*shouldn't want*—to examine?

'Hi, Lexi,' one of the nurses called out to her.

'I just bought my tickets for the ball. I can't wait. You should see the mask I bought online. It's fabulous.'

Lexi's face felt like she was cracking half-dry paint when she smiled. 'Great!'

The ball was the thing she was supposed to be focussed on, not Sam Bailey. It was the event of the year and she was solely responsible for it. It was no secret that some people at SHH were sceptical over whether she would be up to the task. Rumours of nepotism abounded, which made her all the more determined to prove everyone wrong. The proceeds she raised would go to the transplant unit for the purchase of a new state-of-the-art heart-lung bypass machine. Government funding was never enough. It took the hard work of her and her fundraising team to bring to the unit those extras that made all the difference for a patient's outcome.

And her older sister Bella was one of those patients.

Lexi pushed open the door of Bella's room, a bright smile already fixed in place. 'Hi, Bells.'

'Oh, hi, Lexi…' Bella said, her voice sagging over the weight of the words.

Lexi could always tell when Bella had just finished a session with the hospital physiotherapist. She looked even more gaunt and pale than usual. Her sister's thin, frail body lying so listlessly on the bed reminded her of a skeleton shrink-wrapped in skin. She had always found it hard to look at her older sister without feeling horribly guilty. Guilty that she was so robustly healthy, so outgoing and confident…well, on the surface anyway.

She knew it was hard for Bella to relate to her. It put a strain on their relationship that Lexi dearly wished wasn't there but she didn't know how to fix it. Everything Bella did was a struggle, but for Lexi no matter what activity she tried she seemed to have a natural flair for it. She had spent much of her childhood downplaying her talents in case Bella had felt left out. She'd ended the ballet lessons she'd adored because she'd sensed Bella's frustration that she could barely walk, let alone dance. Her piano lessons had gone the same way. As soon as it had become obvious Bella hadn't been able to keep up, Lexi had ended them. It had been easier to quit and pretend disinterest than to keep going and feel guilty all the time.

But it wasn't just guilt Lexi felt when she was around Bella. It was dread. Gut-wrenching, sickening dread that one day Bella was not going to be around any more.

The Lockheart family had lived with that fear for twenty-six years. It was as if the looming shadow of the Grim Reaper had stepped uninvited into their family, and for years had been waiting on the fringes, popping his head in now and again when Bella had a bad attack to remind them all not to take too much for granted, patiently waiting for his chance to step up to centre stage for the final act.

Everyone knew Bella would not reach thirty without a lung transplant. The trouble was getting her healthy and stable enough to be ready for one if a donor became available.

And then there was the waiting list with all those desperately sick people hoping for the same thing: a suitable donor. It was like a weird sort of live-or-die lottery. Even being a recipient of a healthy lung meant that some poor family somewhere else would be mourning the loss of the person they loved.

Life was incredibly cruel, Lexi thought as she put on her happy face for Bella. 'I've brought you a surprise.'

Bella's sad grey eyes brightened momentarily. 'Is it that new romantic comedy everyone is talking about?' she asked.

Lexi glanced at the portable DVD player her sister had on her tray table. Bella was addicted to movies, soppy ones mostly. The shelves the other side of the resuscitation gear held dozens of DVDs she had watched numerous times. 'No, it's not out until next month,' Lexi said. She put the designer shopping bag she'd brought on the bed beside her sister's frail form. 'Go on,' she urged. 'Open it.'

Bella opened the bag and carefully took out the tissue-wrapped package inside. Her thin fingers meticulously peeled back the designer-shop logo sticker keeping the edges together. Lexi was almost jumping up and down with impatience. If it had been her receiving a package the tissue paper would have been on the floor by now in her haste to see what was inside. But

Bella took her time, which was sadly ironic really, Lexi thought, when time was one thing she had so little of.

'What do you think?' she asked as Bella had finally unwrapped the sexy red lacy negligee and wrap set.

Bella's cheeks were about as red as the lacy garments. 'Thanks, Lexi, it was very kind of you but…'

'You need to break out a little, Bells,' Lexi said. 'You're always wearing those granny flannel pyjamas. Passion-killers, that's what they're called. Why not live a little? Who's going to notice in here if you wear something a little more feminine?'

Bella's cheeks were still furnace hot. 'I'm not comfortable in your type of clothes, Lexi. You look stunning in them. You look stunning in anything. You'd turn heads wearing a garbage bag. I'll just look stupid.'

'You don't give yourself a chance to look stunning,' Lexi said. 'You hide behind layers of old-fashioned drab clothing like you don't want to be noticed.'

'Don't you think I get enough attention as it

is?' Bella asked with a flash of her grey eyes. 'I have people poking and prodding me all the time. It's all right for you. You don't have to lie in here and watch the clock go round while another day of your life passes you by. You're out having a life.'

There was a little tense silence, all except for the squeak of a nurse's rubber-soled shoes in the corridor outside as she walked briskly past.

Lexi felt her shoulders drop. 'I'm sorry,' she said. 'I just thought something bright would cheer you up.' She began to collect the lacy items from Bella's lap.

Bella put her hand out to stop her taking away the negligee set. 'No, leave it,' she said on a heavy sigh. 'It was sweet of you. I'll keep it for when I'm better.'

The unspoken words *if I get better* hung in the air for a moment.

Lexi summoned up a smile. 'Actually, I only bought it because there was a two-for-one sale. You should see the little number I bought myself.'

'What colour is it?'

'Black with hot pink ribbons.'

'Are you saving it for your wedding night?' Bella asked.

Lexi averted her gaze. 'I'm not sure…maybe…'

'Have you heard from Matthew?'

'I got an email a couple of days ago,' Lexi said. 'It's hard for messages to get through. His team are building a school in a remote village in Nigeria.'

'I think he's amazing to be volunteering over there,' Bella said. 'He could have just as easily stayed at home in the family business.'

'He'll come back to the Brentwood business once he's done his bit for humanity,' Lexi said.

'It's nice that you're both are so passionate about helping others,' Bella said.

'Yes… ' Lexi dropped her gaze again. 'Oh, and before I forget…' She rummaged in another bag and took out the latest editions of the fashion magazines Bella loved and spread them like a fan on the tray table. 'You should check out page sixty-three in that one. There's a dress design just like the one you drew last week, only yours is better, in my opinion.'

'Thanks, Lexi,' Bella said with a shy smile.

There was the sound of a firm authoritative tread coming down the corridor.

'I bet that's your doctor,' Lexi said, rising from the end of the bed where she had perched. 'I'd better vamoose.'

'No, don't go,' Bella said, grabbing at Lexi's hand. 'That will be the transplant surgeon. You know how much I hate meeting people for the first time. Stay with me? Please?'

There was a cursory knock at the door and then a nurse came in, followed by a tall figure with shoulders so broad they almost filled the doorway.

Lexi felt her stomach hollow out and her heart did that hit-and-miss thing all over again. Could this really be happening to her? What twist of fate had led Sam to be her sister's surgeon? She'd thought he'd planned to be a renal transplant surgeon. She hadn't for a moment suspected he would be Bella's doctor. It would be even harder to avoid him now. There would be ward rounds and consultations in his rooms, follow-ups if the surgery went ahead. Lexi was the one who mostly ferried Bella around. How was she going to deal with being confronted with the pain of her past on such a regular basis?

'Bella,' the nurse said cheerily. 'This is Mr Sam Bailey, the heart-lung transplant surgeon newly arrived from the US. We're very lucky to have someone of his calibre working for us. And lucky you, for you are his very first patient at SHH. Mr Bailey, this is Bella Lockheart.'

Sam held out his hand to Bella. 'Hello, Bella,' he said. 'How are you feeling?'

Bella blushed like a schoolgirl and her voice was nothing more than a soft mumble. 'I'm fine, thank you.'

'And this is Lexi Lockheart,' the nurse continued with a beaming smile as she turned to where Lexi was standing. 'You'll see a lot of her around the place. She's a tireless fundraiser for SHH. If you have spare cash lying around, watch out. She'll be on to you in a flash.'

Lexi cautiously met Sam's gaze. How was he going to play this? As strangers meeting for the first time? Surely he wouldn't acknowledge their previous relationship, not in a place like SHH where gossip ran as fast as the wireless broadband network, sometimes faster. His professional reputation could be compromised if people started to speculate about what had happened between them in the past.

He put out his large, capable hand, the same hand that had once cupped her cheek as he'd leant in to kiss her for the first time, the same hand that had skimmed over and held each of her breasts, the same hand that had stroked down to that secret place between her thighs and coaxed her into her first earth-shattering orgasm. Lexi slowly brought her hand to his, trying to ignore the way his warm palm sent electric zaps all the way to her armpit and back.

'How do you do?' he said in his deep baritone voice.

So it was strangers, then. 'Pleased to meet you, Mr Bailey,' she said, keeping her expression coolly polite. 'I hope you settle in well at SHH.'

'I'm settling in very well, thank you,' he said, his eyes communicating with hers in a private lock that made her flesh tingle from head to foot.

She slipped her hand out of his and stepped back so he could speak to Bella. Her hand fizzed and tingled and she shoved it behind her back as she watched as he interacted with her sister with a reassuring mix of compassion and professionalism.

'I've been going over your history in a lot of detail, Bella,' he said, 'especially your lung function over the last couple of years. I guess I don't have to tell you that there's been significant deterioration.'

Bella's grey gaze looked shadowed with worry. 'Yes, I've been admitted to hospital more often with chest infections and it takes longer and longer to clear things up. I've only just started to improve and I've been in here almost three weeks.'

Sam gave an understanding nod. 'I've looked at your latest CT scans and lung function studies. The lungs are very scarred. That's making them stiff, so it's no wonder you're struggling to breathe when you exert yourself or when you get even a minor infection.'

Bella bit her lip and dropped her gaze to the magazines on her tray table. It was a moment before she looked up at Sam. 'Am I getting to… to the end? How much time do I have left?'

Sam gave her thin shoulder a gentle squeeze.

'We're getting to the stage of needing to do a lung transplant within the next couple of months. I've started the active search for a matching transplant donor. If we find one we need to move straight away before you get another bout of pneumonia. We could find a donor in a day, a week or a couple of months. I'm afraid that longer than that and the chances get worse of keeping you well enough to survive the surgery.'

Lexi listened with dread, feeling like a ship's anchor had landed on the floor of her stomach. It was such a massive operation. What if it didn't work? What if poor Bella died on the operating table or soon after? So much of it seemed up to chance: the right donor; whether Bella was well enough at the time to be the recipient; whether she would survive the long operation. So many factors were at play and no one, it seemed, had any control over any of it, least of all Bella.

Bella must have been thinking the very same thing as she said, 'What are my chances of coming through the operation?'

Sam was nothing if not professional and knowledgeable and encouraging in his manner. 'With modern anti-rejection therapy there's better than an eighty-five per cent chance that you'll survive the surgery and live a good-quality life for the next ten years. After that there's not much data, but expectations are that anti-rejection management will continue to improve and that you could end up living a fairly normal life.'

'You're in good hands, Bella,' the nurse said. 'Mr Bailey is considered one of the world's leading heart-lung transplant surgeons.'

Sam acknowledged the nurse's comment with a quick on-off smile as if he was uncomfortable with praise. Perhaps he was worried about operating on someone to whom he had a connection, Lexi thought. Not that he had ever met Bella before, but he had been intimately involved with Lexi. Clinical distance was paramount in life-and-death surgery. A surgeon could not afford to let the pressure of a relationship, no matter how distant or close, interfere with his clinical judgement. She hoped her involvement with him in the past wasn't going to complicate things for Bella.

'I'll keep you informed on things as we go along, Bella,' Sam said. 'You'll stay in the medical ward until your health improves. If a donor becomes available and you're healthy enough, we'll move you across to the transplant unit. Otherwise we'll send you home until something comes up.'

'Thanks for everything, Mr Bailey,' Bella said blushing again. 'I really appreciate you taking me on.'

Sam smiled and gave Bella's shoulder another gentle touch. 'Hang in there, Bella. We'll do all we can to get you through this. Just try and keep positive.'

He gave Lexi a brief impersonal nod as he left with the nurse to continue his rounds.

Lexi didn't even realise she was holding her breath until Bella looked at her quizzically. 'It's not like you to be so quiet when there's a handsome man in the room,' she said.

Lexi felt her face heating and tried to counter it with an uppity toss of her head. 'He's not that handsome.'

Bella raised her brows. 'You don't think? I thought you had a thing for tall muscular men with dark brown eyes.'

Lexi gave a dismissive shrug. 'His hair is too short.'

'Maybe he keeps it short for convenience,' Bella said. 'He's in Theatre a lot. Any longer and it would get sweaty under the scrub hat during long transplant operations.'

Lexi made a business of folding each sheet of the tissue paper into a neat square, lining them up side by side on the bed.

'He's got nice eyes, don't you think?' Bella said.

'I didn't notice.'

'Liar, sure you did,' Bella said. 'I saw you blush. I've never seen you blush before. That's my specialty, not yours.'

'It's hot in here,' Lexi said, fanning her face for emphasis. 'How do you stand it?'

'Did you notice his hands?' Bella asked.

'Not really...' Lexi remembered how those hands had felt on her body. How they had lit fires under her flesh until she had been burning with a need so strong it had totally consumed her. Those hands had wreaked havoc on her senses from the first moment he had touched her. She opened and closed the hand he had taken in his just minutes ago. The tingling pins and needles feeling was still there...

'He wasn't wearing a wedding ring,' Bella said.

'Doesn't mean he's not involved with someone,' Lexi said, feeling a tight ache in her chest as she pictured his partner. Would she be blonde, like her, or brunette? Or maybe a redhead like Bella. Would she be a doctor or nurse? Or a teacher perhaps? A lawyer? 'Dad's got a new girlfriend,' she said, to change the subject.

'Yes, Evie told me.'

'I haven't met her yet.'

'I don't know why he bothers introducing them,' Bella said with an air of resentment. 'None of them stay around long enough for us to get to know them.'

'Dad's entitled to have a life,' Lexi said. 'It's not like Mum's ever going to come back and play happy families.'

'You always defend him,' Bella said irritably. 'You never let anyone say a bad word about him.'

'Look,' Lexi said, hoping to avoid the well-worn bone of contention between them. 'I know he's not perfect but he's the only father we have. The only parent when it comes down to it. Mum's not much use.'

'Maybe Mum couldn't handle Dad's philandering,' Bella said. 'Maybe it wasn't just because I was sick. Maybe she was left on her own too much and couldn't cope. Maybe she wouldn't have left if he had offered her more emotional support.'

Lexi knew Bella felt terribly guilty about the breakdown of their parents' marriage. Her illness had taken its toll on everyone, but their mother had been the first to abandon ship, taking the contents of the drinks cabinet with her. Miranda Lockheart flitted in and out of their lives, not staying long enough to offer any stability or support but just long enough to remind them of what they had missed out on.

But blaming their father was not something Lexi had ever felt comfortable doing. He had always been there for her. He was her stronghold, the person she looked up to, the person she craved approval from more than any other.

'Dad has always tried to do his best,' she said. 'He was meant to be a father, not a mother. He couldn't do both.'

Bella gave a weary sigh. 'One day you're going to find out that Dad has clay feet. I just hope I'm around to see it.'

Lexi shrugged and then tried another subject change. 'Have you had any other visitors?'

'Phone calls or texts mostly,' Bella said with a despondent look on her face. 'People get sick of visiting after the first week. It happens every time. Maybe it'll be different once I've had the transplant...'

Guilt struck at Lexi like a closed fist. 'I'm sorry I didn't get in yesterday,' she said. 'Matthew's mother wanted me to look at wedding-cake designs. Her sister has already made the cake. Now we just have to decide on the decoration. Matthew wants something traditional but I was thinking we could so something more along the lines of...'

Bella was frowning as she looked into space. It was as if she hadn't heard a word of what Lexi had been saying. 'Sam...' she said. 'Sam. It's really been bugging me. Why does that name sound so familiar?'

Lexi felt her stomach drop again. 'Sam's a popular name.'

'I know but it's more than that,' Bella said, frowning in concentration. 'Bailey. Sam Bailey. Bailey. Sam Bailey.'

Lexi closed her eyes. *Please, no.*

'Oh. My. God.'

Lexi winced as she opened her eyes to see Bella's saucer-like ones staring at her. 'Wh-what?' she choked.

'It's him, isn't it?' Bella asked. 'It's the same Sam Bailey. The Sam Bailey you had that naughty little teenage fling with that made Dad almost blow a fuse. Oh. My. God.'

'Will you please keep your voice down?' Lexi hissed.

'It's not like you'll be able to keep it a secret,' Bella said. 'Not for long and certainly not around here. People have long memories and they just love a bit of juicy gossip. You'd better let Matthew know. You don't want him getting into a flap about an ex-lover turning up out of the blue.'

Lexi turned away to look out of the window, crossing her arms over her body as if that would contain the pain that was spreading like an ink spill through her. Was she deluded to hope no one would remember their past connection? Who else would link their names and start the gossip all over again? How would she cope with it a second time?

No one knew about the baby.

No one.

At least that secret was safe.

But everything else was out there for everyone to pick over like crows on a rotting carcass. All the intimate details of her brief relationship with Sam would be fodder, grist for the mill of gossip that SHH was renowned for. She would be painted as the Scarlet Woman, the scandalous Lolita who had lured Sam away from his studies at the most pivotal moment in his career.

'Lexi?'

Lexi pulled in a breath and faced her sister. 'It was five years ago,' she said. 'Hopefully no one will even remember what happened back then.'

Bella looked doubtful. 'I still think you should tell Matthew.'

'I will tell him,' Lexi said, breaking out into a sweat. 'I'll tell him it was a stupid little fling that meant nothing.'

Bella chewed at her lip for a moment. 'Is this the first time you've seen Sam since you broke up?' she asked.

'No, I ran into him in the doctors' car park on my way to see you,' Lexi said, raking a distracted hand through her hair. 'That'll teach me for breaking the rules. I won't park there ever again. Cross my heart and—' She stopped and gave Bella an apologetic grimace as her hand dropped back by her side. 'Sorry, bad choice of words.'

Bella continued to look at her with a concerned frown on her face. 'You're not happy about seeing him again, are you?' she said.

Lexi lifted her shoulders in a couldn't-careless manner. 'It's always a little difficult running into ex-partners. It's part of the dating life. Once a relationship ends you don't always end up the best of friends.'

'Not that I would know anything about the dating life…' Bella said as she fiddled with the edge of the sheet covering her thin little body.

Lexi sighed and reached for Bella's small, cold hand. 'You're being so wonderfully brave about all this,' she said. 'If it was me I'd be terrified.'

'I *am* terrified,' Bella said. 'I want what you

have. I want a life. I want to one day get married and have babies.'

Lexi felt her insides clench like the snap of a rabbit trap. That aching sadness gripped her every time she thought of the baby she could have had if things had been different. It was ironic that Matthew was keen to start a family as soon as they were married. His parents were excited at the prospect of becoming grandparents. But she had come to dread the topic every time he raised it. It wasn't the only thing she argued with him about. Her lack of interest in sex had become a huge issue over the last few months of their engagement. Matthew's trip abroad, she suspected, were his attempts to make her heart grow fonder in his absence. She didn't have the heart to tell him it wasn't working. She missed him certainly, but not in the way he most wanted her to.

'I'll be the only Lockheart sister left childless and lonely on the shelf,' Bella continued to bemoan.

'Is Evie seeing someone?' Lexi asked feeling a little piqued that she hadn't been told by Evie herself. 'I was under the impression there's been no one since she broke things off with Stuart… what was it? Two years ago?'

'I heard one of the nurses talking about Evie and Finn Kennedy,' Bella said.

Lexi laughed. 'Finn Kennedy? Are you out of your mind? He's the last person I would have picked for Evie. He's so grumpy and brooding. I don't think I've ever seen him smile.'

'He's very kind to patients,' Bella said in his defence. 'And he's smiled at me lots of times.'

'In my opinion Finn Kennedy has a chip on his shoulder that it'd take an industrial crane to shift,' Lexi said. 'I hope to goodness Evie knows what she's doing. The last thing we need in the Lockheart family is another difficult person to deal with.'

There was a small silence.

'Has Mum been in to see you?' Lexi asked.

Bella's shoulders slumped a little further as she shook her head. 'You know what she's like…'

Lexi gave Bella's hand another little squeeze. 'I wish I could change places with you, Bells,' she said sincerely. 'I hate seeing you suffer... I hate the thought of losing you.'

Bella gave her a wobbly smile. 'I guess that's in Sam Bailey's hands now, isn't it?'

CHAPTER THREE

IT WAS a week later when Lexi ran into Sam again—literally. She was coming out of the hospital cafeteria with a latte in one hand while she texted a message on her phone in the other when she rammed into his broad chest. It was like stepping into a six-foot-two brick wall. The coffee cup lid didn't survive the impact and the milky liquid splashed all over the front of Sam's crisp white shirt.

He let out a short, sharp expletive.

Lexi looked up in horror. 'Oops, sorry,' she said. 'I didn't see you. I was…um, multitasking.'

He plucked at his shirt to keep it away from his chest. 'This is a busy hospital, not a social networking site,' he said.

Lexi put up her chin. 'If you had looked where you were going, you could've avoided me,' she shot back.

'You could've burned me,' he said.

'Did I burn you?'

'No, but that's not the point.'

'It is the point,' she said. 'There's no damage other than a stained shirt, which I will take full responsibility for.'

He gave her a mocking look. 'You mean you'll hand it to one of the Lockheart lackeys to launder for you?'

Lexi ground her teeth as she looked up at him. Why today of all days had she worn ballet flats? He seemed to tower over her and it put her at a distinct disadvantage. She was faced with his stubbly chin and had to crane her neck to reach his chocolate-brown eyes. 'I'll see to it that your shirt is returned to you spotless,' she said.

'I can hardly take it off and give it to you in the middle of the busiest corridor of the hospital,' he pointed out dryly.

'Then we'll have to arrange a handover time,' she said. 'What time do you finish today?'

He scraped a hand through his hair. 'Look, forget about it,' he said. 'I have my own laundry service.'

'No, I insist,' Lexi said. 'I wasn't looking where I was going.'

'I'm sure you have much better things to do than wash and iron my shirt,' Sam said.

'Like paint my nails?' she said with an arch look.

He shifted his mouth from side to side. 'OK, round one to you,' he said. 'I had no idea you were so actively involved in raising funds for the unit.'

'I did tell you I was Head of Events.'

'Yes, but I didn't know you had been responsible for raising over five hundred thousand dollars last year.'

'I'm going to double that by the end of this year,' Lexi said. 'You can make a donation if you like. I'll give you the website address. You can pay online. All donations over two dollars are tax deductible.'

Sam was starting to see why she had been chosen for the job. Who could resist her when she laid on the Lockheart charm? She looked especially gorgeous today. She was several inches shorter than usual. But she still smelled as delicious as ever. That intriguing mix of flowers and essential oils teased his nostrils. She was dressed in grey trousers and a loose-fitting white cotton shirt with a camisole underneath that hugged her pert breasts. She had dangling earrings in her ears; they caught the light every now and again, making him think of the sun sparkling on the ocean. It had been her brightness that had attracted him like a moth to a flame all those years ago. He had been drawn to her bubbly nature; her positive outlook on life was such a contrast to his more guarded, introverted approach. She had flirted with him outrageously at a charity dinner held by her father in honour of the hospital. Sam hadn't realised who she was at the time, and he often wondered if he would have taken things as far as he had if he had known she was Richard Lockheart's youngest daughter. He couldn't answer that with any certainty, even now.

Put simply, she had been utterly irresistible.

With her stunning looks, charm and at-ease-in-any-company personality, he had temporarily lost sight of his goal. He had compromised everything to be with her because that was the effect she'd had on him.

But finding out the truth about how she had used him had made him cynical and less willing to open his heart in subsequent relationships. He dated regularly but commitment was something he avoided. Friends of his were marrying and having families now but he had no plans to join them any time soon. He didn't want to end up like his father, loving someone so much that he couldn't function properly without them.

His gaze drifted to Lexi's sparkling engagement ring. He felt a ridge come up in his throat as he pictured her walking down the aisle towards that nameless, faceless man. She would be smiling radiantly, looking amazingly beautiful, blissfully happy to be marrying the man she loved.

Engaged.

The word was a jarring reminder.

Lexi was engaged.

The three words were a life sentence.

Sam gave himself a mental shake. 'I'll get my secretary to make a donation on my behalf,' he said. 'Now, if you'll excuse me…' He pushed against the fire-escape door with his shoulder.

'There is a lift, you know,' Lexi said.

'Yes, I know, but I prefer the exercise.'

She glanced at the lift again before returning

her gaze to where Sam was holding the fire-escape door open. She gave him a tight little smile that had a hint of stubbornness to it and brushed past him to make her way up the stairs. He felt his body kick start like a racing-car engine when her slim hip brushed against his thigh. It was probably not deliberate as there wasn't a lot of space to spare. She went ahead of him up the stairs, another bad idea in spite of it being chivalrous on his part. He got a perfect view of her neat bottom and long legs as she made her way up. He tried not to think of those long legs wrapped around him in passion and that beautiful hair of hers flung out over his pillow.

He had lain awake for the last week, sifting through every moment he had spent with her five years ago. From the very first second when her blue gaze had met his across that crowded room he had felt the lightning strike of physical attraction. It had rooted him to the spot. He had felt like a starstruck fan meeting their idol for the first time. He had barely been able to string a few words together when she approached him. Whatever he had said must have amused her for he remembered the tinkling bell of her laugh and how it had made his skin lift in a shiver.

They had left the gathering together and they had barely surfaced from his tiny flat for the next two weeks. For the first time during his career he had neglected his studies. The thick surgical textbooks had sat on his desk opposite his bed, staring at him in a surly silence. And he had pointedly ignored them while he had indulged in an affair that had been so hot and erotic he could hardly believe it had been happening to him. The physical intensity of it had surpassed anything before or since. He had relished every moment with Lexi in his arms. She had been an adventurous and enthusiastic, even at times playful lover. He suspected she'd had a fair bit of experience, perhaps much more than him, but they hadn't talked about it. Looking back, he realised she hadn't said much about herself at all, even though he had tried to draw her out several times. In hindsight he could see why she had been so reluctant to reveal herself to him emotionally. There had been no emotional commitment on her part. She had simply wanted to create a storm with her father and had used him to summon up the thunderclouds.

'Why did you pretend we didn't know each other last week when you were visiting Bella?' Lexi asked, stopping in mid-climb to look back at him over her shoulder.

Sam almost ran into the back of her. He felt the warmth of her body and got another delicious waft of her perfume. 'I didn't think it was wise to advertise the fact that we'd once been involved,' he said.

'Not good for your career?' she asked with one of her pert looks.

He frowned up at her. 'It has nothing to do with my career. I wasn't sure if your sister knew about us. I'd not met her before. I was playing it safe for your sake.'

'She wasn't at the dinner where we met,' Lexi said. 'But she remembered the dreadful fallout after my father found out we were seeing each other.'

Sam's frown deepened. It had niggled at him a bit that he had never actually seen or spoken to her after her father had approached him with that ultimatum. For the last five years he had just assumed she had run back to the family fortress at her father's bidding. Her little show of rebellion had achieved its aim. She had got her father's attention back solely on her. Back then, Lexi had struck Sam as the type of girl who would never do anything to permanently jeopardise her prized position as Daddy's Little Girl. She would go so far and no further. It was her way of working things to her advantage, or so he had thought.

But what if things hadn't been quite the way her father had said? Lexi had implied on his first day at SHH that she'd had no idea he had gone to the States. Why hadn't she been told where he had gone? Why hadn't she asked? Or had her father deliberately kept her in the dark, perhaps forbidding her to mention Sam's name in his presence, like some sort of overbearing aristocrat father from the past? Was it deluded of him to hope she had invested more in their relationship than her father had suggested? Was it his male pride that wanted it that way instead of feeling like some sort of cheap gigolo who had served his purpose and now meant nothing to her? Had never meant anything to her?

'Your father is well-known for his temper,' he said. 'I hope it wasn't too rough a time for you back then.'

A flicker of something moved over her face but within a blink it was gone, making him wonder if he had imagined it. She gave her head a little toss and turned and continued walking up the fire escape. 'I know how to handle my father,' she said.

Sam followed her up another few steps. 'Why didn't you ask him where I'd gone?' he asked.

He saw her back tighten like a rod of steel before she slowly turned to face him at the fire-escape door. 'Here's the fourth floor,' she announced like a lift operator.

'Why didn't you ask your father, Lexi?' he asked again.

Her blue eyes clashed with his, a spark of cynicism making them appear hard and worldly. 'Why would I do that?' she asked. 'I had a new boyfriend within a few days. Did you really think I was pining after you? Give me a break, country boy. You were fun but not that much fun.'

Sam ground his teeth as he joined her on the

landing, conscious of the tight space and the warmth coming off both of their bodies from the exercise. Lexi's breathing rate had increased slightly, making her beautiful breasts rise and fall behind her camisole. He allowed himself a brief little eye-lock but then wished he hadn't. She was temptation personified. He had never wanted to kiss someone more in his life. Did she know she was having this effect on him? How could she not? He was doing his best to disguise it but there was only so much he could do. He was a red-blooded male after all, and she was all sexy, nubile woman.

He thrust the door open out of the fire escape and nodded for her to go through. She walked past him, this time not touching him. He felt the loss keenly. His body ached to feel her, to touch her, to bring her close against him, to feel every part of her respond to him as she had in the past. It frustrated him that she still had that power over him. It wasn't supposed to be like this now.

Engaged.

Lexi was engaged.

For heaven's sake, why wasn't his body getting the message?

'Is this your office?' she asked as she came to a frosted glass door halfway along the corridor.

'Yes.' He stood at the door, pointedly waiting for her to leave.

She peered past his shoulder. 'Aren't you going to show me around?' she asked.

'Alexis,' he began. 'I don't think—'

'I want your shirt,' she said with a determined look in her blue gaze.

I want your body, Sam thought. He let out a ragged breath. 'I guess I can hardly see patients wearing this,' he said. 'I'll put on some scrubs.'

Lexi followed him into the suite of rooms he had been assigned. He wondered for a moment if she was going to follow him all the way into his office but she perched her neat bottom on one of the seats in the currently unattended reception area and idly leafed through a magazine.

Sam came out wearing theatre scrubs and handed her his shirt. Lexi took it from him and tried to ignore the fact that it was still warm from his body. She wanted to hold it up to her nose to smell his particular male smell but she could hardly do that in front of him. It was perhaps a little foolish of her, sentimental perhaps, but she had never forgotten his wonderful male smell. He hadn't been one for using expensive aftershaves. He had smelt of good clean soap and a supermarket-brand shampoo that had reminded her of cold, crisp apples.

Lexi put the magazine down. 'Look, all other things aside, I just wanted to say thank you for all that you're doing for my sister.'

'It's fine,' he said, his granite face back on. 'It's what I do.'

The silence stretched and stretched like an elastic band pulled to its capacity.

Lexi couldn't stop looking at him. It was as if her gaze was drawn by a force she had no control over. She longed to know what was going on behind the unreadable screen of his dark eyes. Was he thinking of the time they had spent together? Did he *ever* think of it? Did he regret walking away from her without saying goodbye? Why had he gone so abruptly? She had thought he was different from other men. He had seemed deeper and more sensitive, more emotionally available. Or had that all been a ploy on his part to get her into his bed as quickly and as often as he could? It had certainly worked. She had held nothing back from him physically. Emotionally she had been a little more guarded because she'd been worried about revealing how insecure she'd felt as a person. She'd known how unattractive that was for most men. He, like all the other men she had met, had been attracted to her as Lexi the confident and outgoing party-loving social butterfly. She hadn't felt comfortable revealing how much of an act it had been to compensate for the deep insecurities that had plagued her. How being surrounded by people had stopped her thinking about how lonely she'd felt deep inside. She had wanted to wait until she was a little more confident that their relationship had a future before she revealed that side of herself. But he clearly hadn't been thinking about *their* future. His sights had been solely focussed on his own.

'Alexis.' There was a note of warning in his voice.

'Please don't call me that,' she said. 'I know why you're doing it but please don't.'

He turned and walked behind the reception desk, the action reminding Lexi of a soldier going back into the trenches. He fiddled with the computer for a moment before he spoke in a casual tone that belied the tension she could see in the square set of his broad shoulders. 'I didn't realise you hated your name so much.'

'I don't hate my name,' she said. 'It's just I can't get used to you calling me anything but Lexi.'

He stopped fiddling and turned, his gaze colliding with hers. 'Will you stop it, for pity's sake?'

'Stop what?' she asked.

'You know damn well what.'

'I don't know what.'

His hands went into fists by his sides. 'Yes, you do.'

'You mean acknowledging you?' she asked, coming to stand in front of him. 'Stopping to talk to you in the corridor or on the fire escape? Treating you like a person, that sort of thing?'

'You probably staged the coffee thing to get me alone,' he bit out.

Lexi glared at him in affront. 'You think I would waste a perfectly good double-strength soy latte on you?' she asked.

His frown closed the gap between his chocolate-brown eyes. 'That shirt cost me seventy US dollars,' he said through clenched teeth.

She put her hands on her hips. 'If that's so then you need some serious help when you go shopping, country boy,' she tossed back.

'What's that supposed to mean?'

She gave her head a toss. 'Call me if you want a style advisor,' she said. 'I have connections.'

He glared at her broodingly. 'You think I need help dressing?'

No, but I would love to undress you right now, Lexi thought. She reared back from her traitorous thoughts like a bolting horse suddenly facing a precipitous drop. What on earth was the matter with her? Her fiancé was working hard in a remote and dangerous part of a foreign country and here she was betraying him with her wayward thoughts about a man she should have put out of her mind years ago. 'Yes,' she said. 'You need to buy quality, not quantity. That shirt is not stain-resistant. For just fifty dollars more you could have bought a stain- and crease-resistant one.'

'Oh, for heaven's sake,' he said as he rubbed

at the back of his neck. 'I can't believe I'm even having this conversation.'

Lexi headed for the door. 'I'll get this non-stain-resistant, non-crease-resistant shirt back to you as soon as I can but if the stain doesn't come out don't blame me.'

'Careful not to break a fingernail doing it,' he muttered.

Lexi stomped back behind the reception desk, right into his body space, eyes glaring, cheeks hot with anger. 'What did you say?' she asked.

He looked down at her from his height advantage, dark eyes glittering, jaw clenched, mouth flat. 'You heard.'

She stepped forward half a step and stabbed a finger at his rock-hard chest. 'I might be just an empty-headed party girl with nothing better to do than paint my nails in between organising the next shindig, but this unit, your unit, would not be able to do even half of what it does without my help,' she said. 'Maybe you should think about that next time you want to fling an insult my way.'

Suddenly the distance Lexi had been so de-termined to keep between them had closed significantly. She felt a current of energy pass from his body to hers. It was like receiving a pulse of high-voltage electricity through her fingertip. She felt it run all the way up her arm until her whole body was tingling. She felt the shockingly traitorous drumbeat of desire between her thighs. It was a primitive pulse she could not control. The proximity of his hard male body had jolted hers into a state of acute feminine awareness. She could feel every pore of her skin dilating in anticipation. The hairs on the back of her neck rose and danced. A shiver ran down her spine and then pooled at the base, melting her bones and ligaments until she wasn't sure what was keeping her upright. She looked into his eyes, those gorgeous sleep-with-me-right-now-and-be-damned-with-the-consequences eyes and her heart gave an almighty stammer.

He felt it too.

The air was vibrating with the heat of their past sexual history. Every moment she had spent in his arms seemed to have assembled and joined them in his office. Every steaming kiss, every smouldering slide of a hand over her breasts or thighs, every blistering caress that had left her senses spinning like a top.

Every heart-stopping orgasm.

She quickly pulled her hand away from his chest, stepping back blindly. 'I—I have to go…'

She was almost out of the door when he spoke. 'Aren't you forgetting something?'

Lexi turned back, her heart beating like a hummingbird's wings as she met his dark satirical gaze. In his hand was his stained shirt. She hadn't even registered she had dropped it. She stalked back over to him, her mouth set in a grimly determined line. She tried to pluck it from his hand but his other hand came from nowhere and came down on hers, trapping her.

Her breath stopped.

Her heart raced.

Her stomach folded when she looked at his darkly tanned hand covering her lighter-toned one.

Her flesh remembered his. It reacted to his. It flared with heat under his. She could feel the nerves beneath the surface of her skin twitching to fervent life. She could feel the blood galloping through her veins like rocket fuel.

She could feel her self-control slipping.

She moved her fingers within the prison of his, her fingernails scraping him in her panic to be free. 'L-let me go,' she said, but to her shame her voice sounded weak and breathless, nothing like the strident, determined tone she had aimed for.

His eyes held hers in a sensual tussle that made her spine tingle. It seemed like endless seconds passed with them locked together, hand to hand, eye to eye. But then his fingers momentarily tightened before he finally released her.

She stepped back, almost falling over her own feet, flustered and flushing to the roots of her hair. 'How dare you touch me?' she said, rubbing at her hand as if he had tainted her. 'You have no right.'

His eyes glinted smboulderingly. 'I hate to quibble over inconsequential details but you touched me first.'

'I did not!'

He pointed to his chest. 'Right here,' he said. 'I can still feel the imprint of your fingernail.'

Lexi swallowed as his eyes challenged hers. Her heartbeat sounded in her ears, loud and erratic, her breathing even more so. 'You're exaggerating,' she said. 'I barely touched you.'

'One way to find out.'

Her eyes widened as his hand went to the hem of his scrub top. 'What are you doing?' she said hoarsely.

The door behind Lexi opened and a middle-aged woman came sailing in. 'Oh, sorry,' she said. 'Am I interrupting something?'

'No!' Lexi said.

'Not at all, Susanne,' Sam said with an urbane smile. 'Miss Lockheart was just leaving.'

'I don't think I've met you properly before,' Susanne said, offering a hand to Lexi. 'I'm Sam's practice manager, Susanne Healey.'

Lexi put on a polite smile but her voice sounded wooden when she spoke. 'Nice to meet you, Susanne.'

'How are the plans going for the masked ball?' Susanne asked.

Lexi crumpled Sam's shirt into a ball against her chest. 'Fine… Thank you…'

Susanne swung her gaze to Sam. 'I suppose you've offered your yacht to Lexi for the silent auction, have you?'

'Er…no, I—' Sam began.

Susanne swung her gaze back to Lexi. 'You should get him to donate a cruise around the harbour in it,' she said. 'It'd be so popular. Everyone loves a harbour cruise and his yacht is gorgeous. I saw it down at Neutral Bay marina with my husband on the weekend. You could have a champagne lunch. You'll get heaps of bids. Think of the money it'd raise. I'll even put my name down right now. What do you think should be the opening bid?'

Lexi faltered over her reply. 'I—I don't know… two hundred dollars per couple?'

'How does that sound, Sam?' Susanne asked.

Sam spoke through lips that barely moved. 'Fine.'

'You'll have to buy tickets for the ball now, Sam,' Susanne prattled on. 'You can't miss the hospital's most important event of the year. But you must bring a partner. We can't have you dancing all by yourself, can we, Lexi?'

Lexi met Sam's gaze with a flinty look. 'I'm sure Mr Bailey will have no shortage of dance partners,' she said, 'even if he has to borrow someone else's.'

'I wouldn't steal anyone who wasn't already on the make,' he said with an indolent smile.

Lexi felt her cheeks go red-hot but she refused to be the first to look away. She put all the hatred she could into her glare. Her whole body seemed to be trembling with it as it poured out of her like flames leaping from the top of a volcano.

Luckily Susanne had been distracted by the ringing of the phone. She was now sitting behind the reception desk, scrolling through the diary on the computer screen as she spoke to the person on the other end of line. 'No, that should be fine,' she said. 'Mr Bailey is consulting in his rooms that day… Do you have a current referral from your GP? Good. Yes, I'll squeeze you in at five-fifteen.'

Sam raised a dark brow at Lexi. 'You want to continue this out here or take it somewhere a little more private?'

Lexi's eyes flared and her chest heaved with impotent fury. 'Do you really think I would come running back to you at the crook of your little finger?' she snarled at him in an undertone. 'I'm engaged. I'm getting married in less than three months' time.'

His eyes pulsed mockingly as they held hers. 'Is that little reminder for you or for me?' he asked.

'For you, of course,' Lexi said, and swung away, her head high, her cheeks hot, her heart thumping and her stomach an ant's nest of unease, for somehow, even though he hadn't answered, she suspected he'd had the last word.

CHAPTER FOUR

SAM was still sitting at his desk, absently rolling his pen between his fingers, when Susanne announced on the intercom the arrival of Finn Kennedy, the head of department. 'Send him in,' he said.

The door of his office opened and a tall, imposing figure strode in. Even if he hadn't already been aware of Finn's history Sam was sure he would still have been able to tell he had served in the military from the imperious bearing the man exhibited. There was something about the harsh landscape of his face, the commanding air, the take-no-prisoners demeanour and the piercing but soulless blue eyes that spoke of a long career spent issuing orders and expecting them to be obeyed without question.

Brusque at the best of times and reputedly intimidating to many of the junior staff, Finn was a no-nonsense, show-no-emotion type. But

Sam had often wondered if Finn's aloofness had less to do with his personality and more to do with the fact that he had lost his brother while they had both been serving overseas. Finn never spoke of it. If he felt pain or grief or even guilt, he never showed any sign of it.

With a solid background in trauma surgery Finn had retrained to become a highly skilled cardiac surgeon. His formidable manner didn't win him many friends amongst the staff at SHH but his reputation as a dedicated cardiac surgeon was legendary. Unlike most of his colleagues, Finn usually managed to distance his private life from the gossip network. But in the week Sam had been at SHH he had heard rumours of something going on between Finn and Evie Lockheart, Lexi's oldest sister, who was an A and E doctor. But if the rumours were true and Finn was having an affair with Evie, judging from his crusty demeanour, it wasn't going particularly well.

Sam rose from the behind the desk to offer him a hand but Finn waved him back down. 'How are you settling in?' he asked as he sat down in the chair opposite.

'Fine, thanks,' Sam said. 'Everyone's been very welcoming.'

'Accommodation all right?'

'Yes. Thanks for that contact,' Sam said. 'I'm using the same real estate firm to track down a property for me to buy.'

'The press will want an interview,' Finn said. 'You OK with that?'

'Sure,' Sam said. 'I've already spoken to a couple of journalists who've called. They want a photo opportunity but I'm not sure the patient I have lined up is suitable. Bella Lockheart doesn't strike me as the outgoing type.'

Finn grunted. 'Might be her last chance for the spotlight.'

'I hope it's not,' Sam said. 'I'd like to bring her forward on the waiting list but she's got a chest infection. It's a wait and see, I'm afraid.'

Nothing had showed on Finn's face at the mention of the Lockheart name. 'What are her chances?' he asked.

'She needs a transplant within in the next couple of months,' Sam said. He left the rest of the ominous words hanging in the silence.

Still no flicker of emotion on Finn's face.

'We do what we can, when we can, if we can,' Finn said. He rubbed at his arm and then, noticing Sam's gaze, dropped his hand back down to rest along his bent thigh. 'That rumour true about you and the other sister?' he asked.

Sam stiffened. 'What rumour is that?'

Finn's penetrating gaze met his. 'Word has it you and Lexi Lockheart had a thing going five years ago.'

Sam unlocked his shoulder to give a careless shrug. 'We spent a bit of time together, nothing serious.'

Finn gave him a measured look. 'Did her old man have anything to do with you switching to the US training programme?'

Sam frowned. 'What makes you ask that?'

'Just joining the dots,' Finn said. 'You and young Lexi got it on and then a couple of weeks later you were gone. Makes sense that someone had a gun to your head.'

'The truth is I had thought of studying overseas,' Sam said. 'I just wasn't planning to do it right there and then.'

Finn gave a chuckle. 'I'd like to have seen

Richard Lockheart's face when he found out you were sleeping with his youngest daughter.'

'It wasn't a great moment in my life, that's for sure,' Sam said wryly.

'I'm surprised he approved of her fiancé,' Finn said. 'I thought no one was ever going to be good enough for his baby girl.'

Sam swung his ergonomic chair back and forth in a casual manner. 'You know much about her fiancé?'

'Met him at a couple of hospital functions,' Finn said. 'Nice enough chap. Comes from bucketloads of money but he's currently doing a stint with Volunteers Abroad. You see the rock on her finger? He made a big donation to the hospital the day the engagement was announced.' He gave a grunt of amusement. 'Hopefully he'll double it once they're married.'

Sam felt his chest tighten but he forced a smile to his lips. 'Let's hope so.'

'There's a drinks thing organised for Wednesday night at Pete's Bar across the road for you to get to know some of the other departmental staff,' Finn said. 'Just another excuse for the staff to get hammered if you ask me, but you might as well put in an appearance. Half-price Wednesdays are a bit of an institution with the registrars.'

'I got the email about it the other day,' Sam said. 'I'll definitely pop my head in the door.'

Finn stood. 'Right, then,' he said. 'I'm off home. It's been a long day and tomorrow's probably going to be no better.'

Sam stood looking out of the window once Finn had gone. The sun was sinking in the west, casting the city in a golden glow. He had missed that iconic view in the years he had been away. Just knowing it would be there waiting for him to come back had helped quell any momentary feelings of homesickness. But the view had changed, or perhaps his memory of it had.

It just wasn't the same.

On Wednesday evening Sam had been caught up with a particularly tragic case and had spent the extra time explaining the sad prognosis to the patient and his young family.

When he came out to the reception area after dictating the letter to the patient's GP, Susanne drew his attention to a wrapped parcel sitting on the counter. 'That came for you a little while ago.'

'What is it?'

'A shirt,' Susanne said, eyes twinkling. 'From Lexi Lockheart.'

Sam took the package, keeping his expression blank. 'Thank you.'

'She said the stain didn't come out so she bought you a new one,' Susanne said.

Sam frowned at his receptionist's intrigued expression. 'She spilt coffee on it when she bumped into me,' he explained. 'She offered to launder it for me.'

'A little bird told me you and Lexi dated a few years back,' Susanne said, leaning her chin on her steepled fingers.

'Your little bird is wrong because we never actually went out on an official date,' he said, leafing through a pile of correspondence. 'Our entire affair was conducted in private.'

Susanne's pencilled eyebrows lifted. 'I sense some angst between you,' she said. 'That little scene I came in on the other day…'

'Susanne,' Sam said sternly as he put the letters down on the desk, 'I need you to type my letters and schedule my theatre lists and organise my diary for me. I do not need you to speculate on my private life. That is totally off-limits, understood?'

Susanne nodded obediently. 'Understood.'

He was almost out of the door when he stopped and turned to look at her. 'Who was the little bird?' he asked.

Susanne made a buttoning up motion with her fingers against her mouth. 'I promised not to tell. Guide's honour.'

'Oh, for heaven's sake,' Sam muttered and left.

The bar was full and loud with the buzz of conversation and thumping music when Sam finally arrived. He wove his way through the knot of people, saying hello to those he recognised from previous introductions and stopping to greet those who introduced themselves.

Evie Lockheart was one person he remembered from his training years. But as she had been a couple of years behind him in med school they hadn't really socialised. She moved through the crowd and offered a slim hand to him with a polite but contained smile. 'Welcome back to

SHH,' she said. 'I'm not sure if you remember me. I'm Evie Lockheart from A and E. You came to a trainee doctor dinner thing my father held a few years ago.'

Sam took her hand as he returned her smile. Did she also remember he'd only had eyes for her knock-'em-out-gorgeous youngest sister that night as well? And had she been a witness to the fallout Lexi had alluded to? 'Of course I remember you,' he said. 'Nice to see you again.'

'I believe you're doing a great job of looking after my sister,' Evie said.

'Um…pardon?'

Evie smiled to put him at ease. 'I understand patient confidentiality, Sam, but under the circumstances, given we're colleagues, I think it's OK for you to discuss Bella's treatment with me.'

Oh, that sister, Sam thought. 'We're working on getting her well enough to receive a donor lung,' he said. 'She's getting better but finding a match is the next hurdle.'

'We've heard very good things about you,' Evie said. 'Mind you, my father wouldn't have approved your appointment unless he thought you were the best.' She gave him a hard little look. 'Not after what happened between you and Lexi. Talk about World War Three. I thought Dad was going to disown her. I've never seen him so furious with her. I was very worried about her. She took it very hard.'

Sam kept his expression impassive but inside he was reeling. 'Lexi seems very settled now,' he said.

'Yes,' Evie said. 'It's a good match. Matthew is lovely. He's just what Lexi needs. He comes from a very stable family.'

'A very rich family, or so I've been told,' Sam said.

'Mega-rich,' Evie said taking a sip of her drink. 'But unlike some of the silver-spoon set, they're good with it. They support a lot of charities. I think that's why Matthew and Lexi hit it off so well. They have a lot in common.'

Sam wondered what Lexi's fiancé would say if he found out about the tense little scene in his office the other day. Perhaps Lexi was feeling a little frisky with her man away for weeks, if not months, on end. She wasn't the celibate type. She was far too sensual for that. Sam had all the blisteringly hot memories of her to vouch for that.

Finn sauntered over with a glass of single malt whisky in his hand. 'So you finally managed to extricate yourself from the mother ship?' he drawled.

'Yes,' Sam said. 'It's been one of those days. Why is the last patient of the day always the hardest?'

'It's always like that,' Evie said, deliberately turning her body away from Finn as if his presence annoyed her.

Finn's lip curled at the all too obvious snub. 'So how is Princess Evie this evening?' he asked.

Evie gave him an arctic glance over her shoulder. 'There's a new barmaid on tonight, Finn,' she said. 'You might want to see if she's free later on.'

'Maybe I'll do that,' Finn said with a smirk.

The air was crackling with waves of antagonism. It was pretty clear Finn and Evie had something brewing between them but Sam wasn't sure exactly what it was. He had noticed Finn's hand trembling slightly as he brought his drink up to his mouth. He didn't want to think about what had caused that slight tremble. Was that what that arm rub had been about the other day? he wondered. Was that why Evie was so prickly and guarded around him? Did she suspect something but wasn't game enough to put her name and reputation on the line in outing Finn? It was a tough gig reporting a senior colleague and most junior doctors would think twice about doing it.

Being new at SHH would make it equally difficult for Sam. He hadn't been around long enough to be certain but even so, calling out a colleague for suspected alcohol abuse would be nothing short of career suicide. He would only do it if he had enough evidence to prove it was actually the case. There could be any number of contributing factors: extreme tiredness, for instance. He had experienced it himself after long operations and too many nights on call. His whole body had started to quake and tremble with exhaustion. Those symptoms could so easily be misconstrued, and if he was wrong it would have devastating consequences professionally.

Finn Kennedy looked like the overworked

type. His piercing blue eyes were bloodshot, but the damson-coloured shadows beneath them could just as easily suggest a man who was not getting enough sleep rather than a man who was consuming too much of the demon drink. But, then, who could really know for sure?

'You haven't got a drink,' Finn said. 'What would you like?'

'It's OK,' Sam said. 'I'll make my way over now and grab something soft.' He smiled to encompass them both. 'Nice to chat to you.'

Sam was soon handed a drink by one of the registrars and drawn into their circle. He did his best to answer some of the questions fired at him but the whole time he felt strangely disconnected. It was as if his body was standing there talking to the small group surrounding him but his mind was elsewhere. Lexi was just a few feet away. There was a faint trace of her perfume in the air and every now and again he could feel her gaze on him.

'What about harvesting organs?' one of the junior interns asked. 'Do you have to travel to different hospitals to do that?'

'Sometimes, but not to harvest the actual organs I will end up using,' Sam said bringing his attention back to the group in front of him. 'As you know, it's impossible to transfer someone on a ventilator. It's easier for us to go to them once the family has come to the decision of turning off life support. We notify the recipient once the match has been made and then swing into action. There's a lot of co-ordination and co-operation between campuses.'

After a while the conversation drifted into other areas so Sam moved away from the bar to circulate some more. He had only taken a couple of strides when a cluster of people separated and he came face to face with Lexi.

There was an awkward silence.

'Thanks for the shirt,' Sam said gruffly. 'But you shouldn't have bothered.'

'I underestimated the efficacy of my laundering abilities,' she said. 'No matter what I did, the coffee wouldn't come out.'

'You should've just sent it back to me,' he said. 'You didn't need to buy such an expensive replacement.'

'It wasn't expensive. I got it in a half-price sale.'

Another tense little silence passed.

'You know, if you don't want to donate a cruise on your yacht, you don't have to,' Lexi said with a frosty look. 'I have plenty of other people more than happy to donate items much better than yours.'

Sam felt his back come up. 'I didn't say I didn't want to donate it.'

She rolled her eyes in disdain. 'You weren't exactly super-enthusiastic about it.'

Sam frowned at her. 'What did you want me to do? Cartwheels of excitement down the corridor?'

'I didn't even know you had a yacht.'

He threw her a cutting glance. 'Pardon me for the oversight,' he said. 'Would you like a list of the things I currently own?'

She glowered at him. 'I'll need to inspect it at some point,' she said. 'I can't allow it to be used if it's not suitable. I have to consider the public liability issue.'

'Fine,' Sam said. 'Inspect it. I'm sure you'll find it comes up to your impeccable standards.'

'How many people can you fit on board?' she asked.

'I could push it to ten but eight's probably the max for comfort.'

'And what sort of lunch do you plan on offering?' she asked, looking at him in that haughty manner of hers that seemed to suggest she thought he would think a sausage wrapped in a slice of bread and a can of beer would do the job.

Sam stared at her plump, shiny mouth. He couldn't seem to drag his gaze away. She was wearing lip gloss again. He wondered if it was the same one she used to wear. 'Strawberries...'

A tiny frown appeared between her ocean-blue eyes. 'Just...strawberries?' she asked.

Sam had to give himself another quick mental slap. 'Champagne and caviar,' he said. 'You know the sort of deal. Good food, fine wines, gourmet food.'

'I'll look into it and get back to you,' she said. 'What's your boat called?'

'Whispering Waves,' he said. 'It was already named when I bought it.'

'So it's big enough to sleep on?' she asked.

'It sleeps six,' he said, suddenly imagining her

in the double bed beside him, rocking along with the waves. His body stirred as the blood began to thunder through his veins.

He had to stop this—right now.

'I didn't know you were into sailing,' Lexi said. 'You never mentioned it when we…you know…'

'I'd never even been on a yacht before I went to the States,' Sam said. 'I got invited to crew for a friend over there. We did some races now and again. I really enjoyed being out on the water so I decided to buy my own vessel. I had it shipped over before I came back.'

'Do you intend to race over here?' she asked.

'I'm not really into the competitive side of things,' he said. 'I just enjoy the freedom of sailing. I like being out on the water. It's a very different environment from a busy hospital.'

Lexi readjusted the strap of her bag over her shoulder, her gaze drifting away from his. She was aware that people would wonder what they were talking about for so long. 'I'd better let you get back to socialising.'

'You can probably tell I hate these sorts of

gatherings,' Sam said. 'I'm not one for inane chitchat.'

'You just have to get people to talk about themselves,' Lexi said. 'Everybody will say what a great conversationalist you are, but really they're the ones doing all the talking. Believe me, it never fails to impress.'

He tilted his mouth in a mocking smile. 'Does that come from Lexi Lockheart's *A Socialite's Guide to Charming a Crowd*?'

Lexi gave him another wintry look. 'It comes from years of experience talking to people with over-inflated egos,' she said, shifting slightly to one side so one of the residents could make their way past juggling glasses of beer.

'What's going on between your sister and Finn Kennedy?' Sam asked, before she could step any further away.

Lexi looked at him in surprise. 'What? You've heard something too?'

'Not as such,' he said. 'But you've only got to look at them together to see something's going on. They're like two snarling dogs circling each other.'

'So you think that's attraction?'

'I didn't say that,' he said.

'But you think it's a sign.'

'They either hate each other's guts or they can't wait to fall into bed with each other,' he said.

'So that's your expert opinion?' Lexi asked with a cynical look.

He took another sip of his drink before he answered. 'You know what they say about hate and love and the two-sided-coin thing.'

'I think he's totally wrong for her,' she said, frowning.

'Why's that?'

'He's emotionally locked down,' she said emphatically. 'He can't give her what she wants.'

'And you know exactly what she wants, do you?'

Lexi pushed her lips forward as she glanced at her oldest sister. Evie was glaring at Finn, her mouth tight, her eyes flashing as he leaned indolently against the bar with a mocking smile on his handsome face. Lexi frowned as she turned back to Sam. 'I think she wants what every woman wants,' she said. 'She wants a man who loves her for who she is, someone who will protect her and support her but not crush her.'

His brows moved closer together over his eyes. 'You think Finn would crush her?'

'He's got a strong personality,' she said.

'But so does Evie.'

'You sound as if you know her personally.'

'I don't,' he said. 'I've only exchanged a few words with her, but I've heard she's one of the best A and E doctors this hospital has ever seen. I've heard she's ambitious but compassionate. Not unlike Finn.'

'So you think they'd be a perfect match for each other?' Lexi asked with an incredulous look.

He gave a noncommittal shrug. 'I think they should be left to sort out their differences without the scrutiny or judgement of others,' he said.

'That won't be easy in a place like SHH,' Lexi said, chewing at her lip as she thought of what people would make of her and Sam talking at length. If it hadn't been for his wretched shirt and his wretched yacht, she wouldn't have had to speak to him at all.

'Yes, like most hospitals, it's a bit of a hotbed of gossip,' he said. 'I'm surprised people can find the time to work at their jobs when they're so busy spreading rumours.'

'I didn't realise people would talk so much. I didn't realise anyone would even remember that we...' She grimaced. 'I hope it's not too embarrassing for you.'

'It will blow over,' Sam said. 'But to tell you the truth, I'm not sure we could've been any more discreet back then. We kept pretty much to ourselves. I don't think we left my flat for the first ten days. Perhaps if we hadn't ventured out for that take-away meal at the end of our second week, our affair might have gone unnoticed.'

Lexi wondered if he had ever thought about that full-on time over the last five years, the burning-hot lust that had burned like a wildfire between them. The days and nights of passion that had only been interrupted by the necessities of existence—water, sustenance and the minimum of sleep. They had been in such perfect tune with each other physically. It hadn't seemed to matter that they hadn't really known each other. Their bodies had done the talking for them. Each kiss and caress, each stroke of his tongue and each stabbing thrust of his body had revealed to her the truly passionate man Sam was underneath that cool, clinical facade he presented to the world. There was a streak of wildness in him that she suspected few people ever glimpsed. She wondered with a pang of jealousy if he had been like that with anyone else.

She looked into the contents of her glass again as the silence stretched and stretched. 'I shouldn't have lied to you about my age.'

'I shouldn't have believed you,' he said. 'You were too young for me, not just in years but in experience.'

Lexi brought her eyes back to his in surprise. 'So you knew all along?' she asked.

He frowned at her look. 'Knew what?'

She moistened her lips with the tip of her tongue, her gaze slipping away from his. 'Never mind,' she said, wondering if it was her imagination or was every eye in the room on them right at that point? She glanced nervously over her shoulder but everyone was chatting amongst themselves, apart from her sister Evie who was giving her the eye: the older, wiser, big sister look that said, *Be careful*.

Sam glanced at her empty glass. 'What are you drinking?'

'It's all right,' she said. 'I can buy my own drinks.'

'I'm sure you can, but I'm going to get myself a mineral water so in order to be polite I thought I'd ask if you would like a fresh drink.'

She let out a little breath. 'I'm drinking lemon, lime and bitters.'

He hiked up one brow. 'Nothing stronger?'

'I like to keep my head together at things like this,' she said. 'No one likes to see a drunken woman making a fool of herself, be she young or old.'

Sam had heard on the hospital grapevine about Lexi's mother's issue with alcohol. It seemed the burden of taking care of the chronically ill Bella for all those years had led Miranda Lockheart straight to the drinks cabinet. Gin had been her choice of anaesthesia. Sam had met many parents who had done exactly the same thing. He didn't judge them for it. He felt sorry for them. Sorry that there weren't enough supportive people in their life at that point of crisis to help them through without the crutch of other substances.

He brought their drinks back and handed Lexi hers. 'Your sister hinted at the reaction your father had to our affair,' he said. 'She said he almost disowned you. And that it was a very bad time for you. Is that true?'

Lexi looked at her drink rather than meet his penetrating gaze. 'I'd rather not talk about it.'

'Your father was furious with me,' Sam said after a moment of silence. 'He threatened to derail my career. I knew he had the power and the contacts to do it. It wouldn't have been the first time a trainee has been bumped off the training scheme. I decided to transfer my studies. The way I saw it, it was a case of leave or fail. I figured it was the only way to keep myself on track for qualifying. But I didn't realise he had directed his anger at you too. That hardly seems fair when I had already taken responsibility for everything that had happened.'

Lexi felt her heart give an almighty stumble. Could it be true? Had her father threatened him? Was that why he had disappeared without a trace, without even saying goodbye to her? She thought of how furious her father had been with her when he had discovered she had been involved with Sam. It had been the first time she had been on the receiving end of his wrath and it had totally crushed her. She had always been the one who pleased him. It was her role in the family: Daddy's little girl.

Evie was the academically gifted one, the mother substitute who had taken on all the responsibility of looking after the family after their mother had left. The nannies and au pairs their father had organised had had nothing on Evie. She was the go-to sister, the one who had always made sure they got everything they needed.

Bella was the middle one, the chronically sick and incredibly shy child who had not been expected to live past her early twenties, if that. Their father had made it more than clear that he felt repulsed by Bella's sickness and her shyness was another strike against her. He thought it brought shame to the family name to have a daughter who blushed and could barely string two words together in the company of anyone outside the family.

Growing up without a mother on hand, Lexi had idolised her father. She had come to realise that deep down she was terrified he too might leave if she didn't please him. Being a social butterfly was her way of feeling needed. She loved being surrounded by people, and parties were a perfect place to showcase her talent at working a room. Even as young as five she had been able to pass around plates of canapés like an accomplished hostess four times her age. And it had only got better as she'd grown into young womanhood. She had lapped up her father's approval with every event or party she had helped him organise. His praise had been like an elixir she'd needed to survive. It had been the only way to feel close to him.

Maybe Sam was making it up, maybe it wasn't true. Her father would never have gone that far, would he? The memories, long buried deep inside her, bubbled to the surface—her father's fury, how long it had taken her to get back into his good books, what she'd had to do to prevent him finding out about the baby… Suddenly, it felt like she had been betrayed by him in the most devastating way.

Her teeth sank into her bottom lip as she looked up at Sam's face. She had to know. 'Did my father really threaten to end your career?' she asked.

Sam's expression was impossible to read. 'It's not important now, Alexis,' he said. 'It wouldn't have worked out between us anyway. I was too career-oriented to give you the time and attention you needed. It was just a crazy lust-driven fling. I should've had better control.'

Lexi felt a choked-up feeling at the back of her throat as she looked up at him. If only she had known what had been at stake for him. If only she had known he hadn't really had a choice but to leave. It was so heartbreaking to think about what could have been if only she had known what had gone on between him and her father.

Her chest rippled with a spasm of pain. Would their baby have had his dark brown eyes and light brown hair, or would it have had her blue eyes and blonde tresses? Would it have been a girl or a boy? If things had been different, their baby would be in preschool now. He or she would be learning to recognise letters, making friends, finger painting, making things with Play-Doh: all the innocent things of childhood.

Lexi had made her decision based on what she

had known at the time and it had been the hardest thing she had ever done. She had been so frightened of her father's reaction to the news of her pregnancy. She had felt so unprepared for the responsibilities of motherhood. She hadn't been able to talk to anyone about it. She had hidden it from everybody. She hadn't even told her sisters. Not even Evie, who would have surely helped her and guided her. Instead, she had booked herself into a clinic, miles away in the outer suburbs where her name wouldn't be connected with the powerful and influential Lockheart name. She had stoically faced the impersonal removal of Sam's baby, but on the inside she was devastated that she'd had to make such a harrowing decision. The bottomless well of sadness over that time never seemed to ease, no matter how hard she tried to put it behind her.

Lexi was aware that they were still in the bar surrounded by people but she had never felt so utterly alone. It was like a glass wall was around her, a thick impenetrable wall that had locked her inside with her sorrow.

'Why do you keep calling me Alexis?' she

asked. 'I don't understand why you can't call me Lexi like you used to do.'

An irritated frown carved deep into his forehead. 'You know why,' he said. 'We need some distance.'

'How much distance do you want?' she asked. 'I'm based at the hospital and I'm not leaving just because you've flown back into town. You can't pretend it never happened, Sam. It did and nothing you do or say will ever change that.'

The strong column of his throat moved up and down as if he was trying to swallow a boulder. 'Don't do this, Alexis,' he said. 'Don't try and pretend our fling was something it wasn't. You only got involved with me to get back at your father. An act of rebellion, he called it.'

Lexi looked at him with tears burning like acid at the back of her eyes but only sheer willpower prevented them from appearing, let alone falling. Could this possibly get any worse? As if her father's threats against Sam hadn't been enough. Had her father really said that, lied like that? How could the parent she had adored for as long as she could remember deliberately sabotage her relationship with the man she had thought might be the only one for her? It was a devastating blow to see her father in such a light. He had put his own interests ahead of her happiness. What sort of parent did that to their child? 'Is *that* what he told you?' she asked.

He closed his eyes briefly as if this was all a horrible dream and she would disappear when he opened them again. 'I don't want to cause trouble between you and your father,' he said. 'Our relationship wouldn't have lasted either way. We had nothing in common. We were on completely different pathways.'

'You being Mr Ambitious and me being an empty-headed social butterfly with no aspirations beyond shopping and partying?' she asked, emotion bubbling up inside her like scalding lava.

He raked a hand through his hair in a distracted manner. 'Alexis...' He caught her glacial look and amended on an out breath, 'Lexi... '

'You think I didn't have aspirations?' Lexi said bitterly. 'You have no idea. Do you think I didn't want to do well at school and go to university? I could have achieved way more than I did but how could I do that to Bella? Tell me that, country boy. I had a sister two years older than me who ended up in the same class as me at school. She had to stay back because of her illness. How could I outshine her? How do you think that would have made her feel? I had to play down my talents so she could feel good about herself for just a few moments each day. I wanted to do well but she was more important. So don't talk to me about my lack of ambition. Sometimes there are situations that require sacrifice, not ambition at the cost of those you love. I chose the former, so shoot me.'

It was a great exit line and Lexi used it. She pushed past the knot of people blocking the exit and stumbled out into the street. But home was the last place she wanted to be. She wasn't ready to face her father after this evening's revelations.

Right now she desperately needed to be alone.

CHAPTER FIVE

S<small>AM</small> was walking along the corridor after finishing a ward round on the following Monday afternoon when he saw Lexi coming towards him. As soon as she saw him she swiftly turned on her heel and started walking quickly back the way she had come.

'Lexi, wait,' he said, increasing his strides to catch up. 'Can I have a quick word?'

She stopped and turned, sending him a hard little glare. 'I'm on my way to visit Bella.'

'Bella's resting,' he said. 'I've just been in to see her. She's having some oxygen to boost her levels. Just give me a couple of minutes, OK?'

She let out a long hissing breath. 'All right, if you insist.'

'I insist,' Sam said. 'But not here in the corridor.' He pushed open the door of the on-call room and waited for her to go in.

Lexi brushed past him with her head at a

haughty angle. 'This had better not take long,' she said.

'It won't, I promise.'

Sam closed the door and allowed himself the luxury of sweeping his gaze over her. She was breathtakingly beautiful, dressed in corporate wear that on another woman could have looked conservative and boring but on her looked absolutely stunning. The prim white blouse hugged her breasts and the narrow skirt teamed with high heels gave her a sexy secretary look that was distinctly distracting. Her perfume drifted towards him as she folded her arms across her body and a tendril of hair escaped from the neat chignon she had fashioned at the back of her swan-like neck. Everything about her fired his blood to fever pitch. It was impossible to be in the same room as her and not want to take her in his arms and kiss her senseless.

His body remembered every contour and curve of hers: her sensual mouth and the way it had fed so hungrily off his; her soft hands with their dancing fingertips that had set his skin on fire; the way her long, slim legs had wrapped around his waist as he'd plunged into her hot moistness;

the way her body had gripped him tightly as if she'd never wanted to let go; the way her hips had moved in time with his, her breathing just as frantic as his own gasps; the way her platinum-blonde hair had spread like a halo around her head in the throes of passion; and the way she had gasped his name, her body convulsing in ultimate pleasure, triggering his own cataclysmic release. No matter how hard he tried he couldn't remove the memory of her touch from his mind, much less his body. She wore another man's ring but, heaven help him, he still wanted her.

She tapped her foot on the floor impatiently. 'Well?'

Sam let out a long breath. 'Lexi, I owe you an apology. I should've come to see you before I left for the States. It was wrong of me to just up and leave like that. I didn't think about your end of things at all. I just believed what your father said about you and left it at that. I realise now that I should've at least listened to your side.'

Her blue eyes were still hostile, the set of her shoulders stiff with tension. 'Is that all?'

'No, it's not all,' Sam said. 'I took on board

what you said about the sacrifices you've made to protect Bella.'

She didn't move or speak, just stood there watching him silently, accusingly.

Sam took another breath and slowly released it. 'I should've realised the adjustments you've had to make,' he said. 'I know more than most how the squeaky wheel gets the oil in families and how other siblings can feel left out or isolated as a result.'

'Fine,' Lexi said. 'Can I go now?'

Sam frowned. 'You're not making this easy on me.'

Her eyes hit his like blue diamonds. 'Why should I?'

'You're right,' Sam said, letting his shoulders down on a sigh. 'Why should you?'

He was still trying to get his head around this new Lexi. Not the party girl but the young woman who loved her sister so much that she put her own interests to one side. It went against everything she had told him about herself back then. During their short fling she had laughed off his comments about her lack of ambition. She had said how much she loved the social circuit, how all she had time for was fun, not boring old stuffy studying. Those had been her exact words. He had thought at the time it was such a waste given that he'd had to work so hard to get to medical school.

Unlike Lexi, he hadn't gone to a fee-paying school with the best resources on hand. He had toughed it out in the bush in between helping his father run their drought-ravaged sheep property. He had missed days, sometimes weeks of school to help nurse his mother through the last stages of her kidney disease. Catching up with his studies had been an added burden eclipsed by worry about his mother's declining health and the quiet desperation he'd seen in his father's sun-weathered face whenever he'd looked at his wife lying listlessly in the bedroom of the run-down homestead.

Hearing Lexi say she had deliberately sabotaged her educational achievements to protect her sister was something that had touched Sam deeply. It had made him take pause. He had not realised what a compassionate person she was. Her shallow party-girl persona was a clever artifice for a sensitive young woman who clearly suffered a lot of survival guilt. She had thrown herself into fundraising for SHH, but what else would she have secretly loved to have done? What dreams and aspirations had she put to one side in order to protect her sister from feeling inadequate?

It was part of his job to deal with the families of transplant patients. He understood the dynamics, the sometimes tricky family situations that fed into the patients' outcomes, whether they liked it or not. He wanted to do a good job on Bella, not just because she was Lexi's older sister but because she was a deserving recipient of a lung donation. But even more than that he wanted to make sure Lexi got her chance to shine. Operating on her sister could well be the most important transplant he had ever performed.

Sam looked at her standing there with a mutinous expression on her beautiful face. Anyone seeing her now would assume she was a sulky spoilt brat but he felt like the scales had been removed from his eyes. He could see the hint of vulnerability in her ocean-blue gaze and the almost imperceptible quiver of her bottom lip, as if she was holding back a storm of emotions. 'Why did you get involved with me?' he asked. 'Why me and not someone else?'

'It wasn't an act of rebellion,' she said. 'It was nothing like that.'

'Then what was it?'

She unfolded her arms and used one of her hands to brush back her hair. 'I can't explain why,' she said. 'It just…it just happened.'

Sam watched as she moved restlessly to the other side of the room, her arms folded protectively across her body. Her cheeks were a delicate shade of pink as if the memory of their time together unsettled her more than she wanted to admit. Her saw her beautiful white teeth sink into the soft fullness of her bottom lip. It was one of her most engaging habits, one he suspected she was largely unaware of. It gave her a look of innocence and guilelessness; the potent mix of sexy woman and innocent girl was totally captivating.

'At the pub the other night you said something that's been niggling at me ever since,' he said. 'What was it you thought I'd always known about you?'

Lexi kept her gaze out of the range of his. 'It doesn't matter now...'

But of course he wouldn't leave it at that. 'It was when I mentioned that we'd been worlds apart in years and experience,' he said. 'Tell me, Lexi. What was it you thought I'd always known about you?'

She pressed her sandpaper-dry lips together. Her throat felt tight, too tight even to swallow. Her stomach was churning so much she could hear it rumble in the prolonged silence. Why had she even mentioned it? What was the point of going over this now?

It was over.

They were over.

She was moving on with her life.

Or trying to...

'Lexi?'

His commanding tone summoned her gaze. 'I didn't just lie about my age,' she said on an expelled breath.

His gaze never wavered; it remained rock-steady on hers, but the darkness of his eyes seemed to deepen another shade. 'What else did you lie about?'

She moistened her lips in order to get them to move again in speech. 'Actually, it wasn't really a lie, not an outright one. It was just that I didn't quite tell you the truth.'

Sam's forehead became a map of frowning lines. 'The truth about what?'

Lexi took a breath and then released it in a rush. 'I was…I was… You were my first lover.'

His face looked as if it had just received an invisible slap. She saw him flinch, every muscle contracting, his eyes widening and his mouth opening and closing as if he couldn't quite locate his voice. *'What?'*

'I was a virgin.' Lexi bit her lip. 'At least technically I was…'

'Technically?' he asked. 'What the hell is that supposed to mean?'

She pulled in another uneven breath. 'I'd had boyfriends in the past,' she said, 'lots of them actually. I just hadn't…you know…done it…gone all the way…'

Sam raked his fingers through his hair as he paced back and forth. 'I can't believe I'm hearing this.' He stopped to glare at her furiously. 'Why on earth didn't you say something?'

'Because I knew if I'd said something you wouldn't have slept with me.'

'You're damn right I wouldn't,' he said. 'What were you thinking, Lexi? You were just a young girl. We had so much sex over those two weeks.' His throat moved up and down over a tight swallow. 'Did I…did I hurt you?'

She shook her head vigorously, perhaps too much so.

'Lexi?' He barked her name at her.

'All right, all right,' she said, her eyes rolling in defeat. 'Just a little bit but it was fine after the first—'

'Oh, dear God,' he said, rubbing a hand over his face.

Lexi stalked to the other side of the room. 'You're making such a big deal out of this,' she said. 'I had to lose my virginity some time. At least it was with a considerate lover. It could've been a lot worse.'

He glared at her again. 'How much worse could it have been? I thought I was sleeping with an experienced party girl who knew all the rules,' he said. 'Now I find out she was an innocent virgin.'

'Not so innocent,' Lexi put in.

He held his head in both of his hands and groaned. 'No wonder your father was ready to nail me to the floor.'

'My father didn't know I was still a virgin,' she said. 'It's not exactly something you discuss over the dinner table.'

'No, but it *is* something you discuss with a potential sexual partner,' he pointed out.

'Not when you're having a meaningless, short-term fling,' she threw back.

He stilled. Not a muscle moved. He was like a statue, frozen. 'So,' he said finally in a voice undergirded with steel. 'Let me get this straight. You just wanted a meaningless short-term fling and I was the handiest candidate. Is that right?'

'No...'

'For heaven's sake, Lexi,' he said bitterly, his voice a harsh rasp of anger. 'You nearly cost me my career. I almost lost everything because of you. Do you realise that? Did you even think about what the consequences would be?'

Lexi turned away from his thunderous expression, her arms going back across her body, tightening like a band to hold herself together. He was a fine one to talk about consequences. He hadn't had to face the biggest consequence of all. 'It wasn't like that,' she said.

'What was it like, damn it?' he asked.

She let out a shaky breath. 'When we met…I felt something.'

'Lust.' There was no mistaking the disdain in his voice.

She threw him a look. 'Not just lust. Before you came along I didn't feel ready for a relationship, not a sexual one at least. But it was different with you. From the first moment we met…'

His eyes hardened to chips of ice. 'Don't,' he said, a warning thread of steel in his tone.

'Don't what?'

'Don't try and dress up what we felt for each other as anything other than what it was,' he said. 'I know it's not the most romantic fact in the world but sometimes sex just happens because of instinct. Chemistry. Animal lust.'

'It wasn't like that for me,' Lexi said quietly.

'Well, it was like that for me,' he snapped back.

Lexi turned away again, not willing to let him see how much he had hurt her. She had hoped… foolishly hoped that he had felt something for her back then, but their brief relationship had meant nothing to him.

She had meant nothing to him.

She had just been another name in his little black book. It was deluded of her to have expected anything else. His career was his priority. It had been back then and it still was now. She had been a temporary distraction that he deeply regretted. The breathtaking magic of their relationship that she had revisited so many times in her mind was an illusion, a flight of fancy on her part, romantic nonsense that had no place in the cold, hard world of reason. Emotion clogged her throat, a cruel strangulation of regret and recriminations. Tears were so close she had to blink to stop them from falling. The tattered remnants of her pride would not allow her to cry in front of him.

She made a move for the door. 'I have to go…'

'Hang on a minute,' Sam said. 'We haven't finished this discussion.'

Lexi slung the strap of her bag over her shoulder from where it had slipped. 'I think we have, Sam. There's nothing more to be said.'

'Wait.'

He caught her arm on the way past, his fingers like a metal band around her wrist as he swung her back to face him, the sudden movement sending a shockwave through her body.

The skin on her wrist sizzled as if he had branded her with his touch. His long, strong fingers were like fire. They burned through the layers of her skin, setting nerves into a crazy, maniacal dance. She felt the strength of his grasp as she tried to pull away and her heart started to pound like a faulty timepiece.

She breathed in the scent of him, the hint of aftershave overridden by the sexy musk of late-in-the-day male. She could see the pinpoints of stubble on his jaw and her fingertips tingled as she remembered how it felt to stroke that sexy regrowth with her own soft skin.

Her lips, too, remembered how it felt to move over that bristly surface. She wanted to do it now, to remind herself of how he tasted. She wanted to feel her tongue lapping at his skin the way she had in the past.

Lexi looked into his dark, mesmerising eyes and it was like looking into them for the very first time. She felt the same electric shock rush through her, making every single pore of her body acutely aware of him. The raw physicality of it terrified her. It shocked her that her body could want one thing while her mind insisted on another.

Her leg wasn't supposed to be moving forward half a step to bring her body up against the rock wall of his.

Her breasts weren't supposed to be pressed against his chest, the nipples already tightly budded with desire.

Her pelvis wasn't supposed to be anywhere near his, certainly not flush against him and shamelessly responding to the hard ridge of his growing arousal.

Her inner core was pulsing with a longing that felt so intense, so rampantly out of control it was like a fever in her blood.

It was wrong.

Forbidden.

Dangerous...

She dropped her gaze to his sexily sculpted mouth. It was suddenly just a breath away from hers as if her lips had drawn his down through a force of their own. She could see each of the fine vertical creases in his lips, the masculine dryness an intoxicating reminder of how it felt to have his mouth possess her soft, moister one. She could feel the mint-fresh breeze of his breath as it skated across her lips. It was like a feather teasing her, stirring every sensitive nerve until she thought she would go mad if he didn't cover her mouth with the heated pressure of his to assuage the spiralling need.

His mouth moved infinitesimally closer.

Lexi felt his erection, so thick, so powerful and so wickedly tempting against her. She pulled a breath into her lungs but it felt as if she was hauling a road-train along with it. All she had to do was step up on tiptoe and press her mouth to his…

'If you don't step back right now I'm going to do something I swore I wouldn't do,' Sam said in a deep, rough burr that sent a shiver down her spine.

'Why don't *you* step back?' Lexi asked, not because she wanted to win this particular battle but more because she couldn't get her legs to work right at that moment.

'Don't do this, Lexi,' he said, still staring at

her mouth, his breath a warm caress on her lips, his body still hot and heavy and aroused against hers.

Lexi felt the hammering of his heart beneath her palm where it was resting on his chest. Its pace was just as hectic and uneven as hers. His hands were gripping her by the upper arms, his warm fingers scorching her flesh. She felt the battle raging in the pulse of his blood, pounding through his fingertips, the war between holding her tighter and letting her go. 'You touched me first,' she said. 'You grabbed my arm.'

'I know,' he said in a gravelly voice. 'It was wrong. I shouldn't have touched you. I don't want this complication right now.'

'So step back.'

His glittering eyes seared hers for a pulsing moment. 'You're enjoying this, aren't you?' he said. 'You're enjoying the fact that you still have this effect on me.'

'You want me to step back?' she asked with a pert look. 'Then let go of my arms.'

His fingers loosened but he didn't release her. 'When I'm good and ready,' he said. And then he brought his mouth down slowly, inexorably towards hers.

Lexi knew she should have moved. She knew she should have pushed against his chest and put some distance between their bodies. She knew she should not have just stood there waiting for his mouth to come down to hers. She knew it, but in that moment she was trapped by her own traitorous need to feel his lips against hers just one more time.

As soon as his lips met hers she felt the electric shock of it through her entire body. It travelled from the sensitive surface of her lips to the innermost core of her where that deep ache of longing was flexing and coiling. Hot pulses of need fired through her as her lips felt the subtle pressure of his. He kept the kiss light at first, experimental almost, as if he was rediscovering the landscape of her lips. It started with a brief touchdown of hard, cool lips on her softer ones. A barely touching brushstroke and then another. He raised his mouth off hers a mere fraction but her lips clung to the rougher surface of his. He pressed down again, slightly harder this time, his lips moving against hers in a gentle exploration.

But then it all changed.

That one searching stroke of his tongue against the seam of her mouth made the kiss became something else entirely. Lexi opened to his command, hungrily feeding at his mouth, brazenly playing with the stab and thrust of his tongue. It was a kiss of passion, of unmet desires, frustration and, yes, maybe even a little bit of anger thrown in for good measure. She tasted the wonderful familiarity of him, a hint of mint, good-quality coffee and that unmistakable maleness she had missed so very much. His tongue was roughly masculine against the softness of hers, stirring in her deep yearnings for the physical completion she had only felt with him.

Being back in his arms felt so right, so perfect, the chemistry so hot and electric it was making her blood hum in her veins. He drew her even closer by placing his hand in the small of her back, a touch full of intimacy and deliciously primal in its intent. She felt the rigid heat of him against her, the unmistakable swelling of his hard male body in response to hers. It was a breathtaking feeling to be back in his embrace, to experience the way her body fitted against the contours of his as if made specifically for him.

His kiss deepened even further as he gave a low growl deep in his throat, and the hand at her back pulled her even closer while his other hand cupped the back of her head, his broad fingers splaying in her hair. Every nerve ending on her scalp fizzed at the contact, sharp arrows of pleasure darting through her from the top of her head to her toes. She had to step up on tiptoe to kiss him back and the movement brought her breasts up against his chest, the friction so wonderful she pressed herself even closer. Below her waist she could feel the hard male ridges of his body, the stark difference that made him so male and her so female.

His mouth continued its sensual assault on hers—hot, moist, urgent, masterful and unbelievably thorough. She kissed him back with all the longing she'd had locked away inside her for five long, heartbreaking years. It was like unleashing a wild beast, and once let loose the unrestrained desire could not be subdued or tamed. Her tongue tangled with his, teasing, flirting and then darting away as he came in search of her.

It was a cat-and-mouse game, a battle of wills, a war between two strong opposing forces.

The hand he had placed at the small of her back shifted to cup her bottom. The pressure of his hand drew her pelvis so close to his she felt the complete outline of his potent erection. She felt her stomach drop like an out-of-control elevator as he moved against her. This was what she remembered so well about him. The way he took charge physically, the way he left her breathless with longing, the way his body told her all she needed to know about what he felt about her.

He still wanted her.

Lexi could feel her mouth swelling from the prolonged kissing. She didn't care. She didn't even care that she tasted a hint of blood. She didn't know if it was hers or his. She didn't want the kiss to end. She linked her arms around his neck, her fingers exploring the thick pelt of closely cropped light brown hair on his head.

No one kissed her like Sam did. It was a sensual assault that made her whole body sing and hum with delight. His kiss was erotic and daring, demanding with that edge of hungry desperation in it that suggested he was only just managing to keep control.

Meanwhile, her own control had slipped way out of her grasp. She knew kissing Sam was wrong while she was wearing another man's ring, she knew it and yet she couldn't stop herself responding to the intoxicating magic of his mouth on hers. It was like a drug she knew was forbidden and dangerous but craved anyway. She didn't care about the moral consequences right now. Now was about feeling the red-hot passion Sam incited in her body. Her flesh was tingling and crawling with the need for more of his touch. Her breasts were aching for the caress of his lips and tongue. Her feminine core was pulsing a primal beat that was reverberating throughout her body. It was an unstoppable desire, a longing for the sensual high of passion that she knew he alone could give her. She pushed against him shamelessly, her mouth locked to the bruising pressure of his, wanting more, needing more, aching for more.

Sam suddenly wrenched his mouth off hers, his hands dropping away from her as if she had burned him. 'That should never have happened,' he said, breathing heavily, the fingers of one hand scoring through his hair in agitation.

Lexi took a moment or two to reorient herself. Her senses were spinning so much she felt as if she had just stepped off a merry-go-round that had been going way too fast. Guilt made her go on the attack. 'You started it.'

'You should have stepped back,' he scolded.

She gave him a challenging look, still not ready to accept the total blame. 'Why didn't *you* step back?'

He let out a stiff curse. 'I told myself I wasn't going to do this,' he said, dragging his hand down over his face until it distorted his features. He dropped his hand and glowered at her. 'We should never have got involved,' he said. 'Not then and certainly not now.'

'Who said anything about getting involved?' she said, waving her hand in front of his face. 'I'm engaged, remember?'

The ringing silence was accusing.

Lexi glared at him, directing the anger she felt at herself onto him instead. 'Do you really think I would become involved with you again?' she asked. 'I'm not that much of a fool. You might be happy spending your life passing from one bed to another like a game of musical chairs, but that's not for me. I want stability and certainty.'

'So you picked the richest man in your circle and got yourself engaged to him,' Sam said with a cynical look.

'You don't have any idea of what I want or who I am,' Lexi flashed back. 'You didn't know me five years ago, and you don't know me know. Not the real me. I was just a girl you wanted to sleep with. You didn't want anything else from me. Sex is easy for men like you. It's just a physical thing. Emotions don't come into it at all. I want more than that now. I want the physical and the emotional connection.'

He continued to look at her with his dark, smouldering eyes. 'Are you going to tell your fiancé about that little physical connection we had just now?'

'Let's just forget about it, OK?' Lexi said, hot in the face, even hotter on the inside where the pulse of longing still hummed like a tuning fork struck too hard. 'As far as I'm concerned, it didn't happen.'

Sam thrust his hands deep in his trouser pockets in case he reached for her again. He was sorely tempted. It would be so easy to haul her back against him and force her to admit the need he could see playing out on her features. He could see the battle she was having with herself. He was having it too. Was it because she was now off-limits that this need was so overpowering? He hadn't felt like this with other partners. Each time he had moved on without a backward glance when the relationship had folded. After a couple of months he hadn't even been able to recall their names. But something about Lexi drew him like a bee to a pollen-laden blossom. He ached for her. A bone-deep ache that was as strong as it had ever been. How long was she going to deny what was still between them? Or was this just a game to her, a way of paying him back for leaving without giving her notice

'Are you happy, Lexi?' he asked.

Her blue eyes met his, wariness, uncertainty shining there. 'What do you mean?'

'With this Matthew guy,' he said. 'Are you sure he's the right one for you?'

A defensive glitter came into her eyes. 'Of

course he's the right one for me,' she said. 'I wouldn't be marrying him if he wasn't.'

'The way you responded to me just then made me think—'

'I don't want to hear this,' she said, swinging away in irritation.

'You can't just ignore what happened,' he said. 'You can't just push it under the carpet.'

'It meant nothing!' she said. 'I just got a little carried away. We both did.'

'Lexi—'

'Stop it, Sam,' she said with a warning glare. 'Just stop it, will you? I want to forget about it. It was a stupid mistake. You're right. It should never have happened.'

Sam strode over to her, right in front of her, so close he could smell her perfume again. So close he could have touched her. So close he could feel her sweet vanilla-scented breath wafting on his face. 'How can you even *think* of marrying that guy when just minutes ago I could have had you up against that wall?' he asked.

Her hand came up in a flash, connecting with his cheek in a hard slap that cracked through the air like a stockwhip.

Sam held himself very still, his eyes locked on hers. The air pulsated with the combined force of their anger. It was a thundercloud of frustration, a hurricane of hatred and longing, a lethal mix that could explode at any moment. He felt the tension in his body. The wires of his restraint were stretched to the limit.

He had never wanted anyone more in his life.

'Feel better now, do we?' he asked.

Her throat rose and fell over a tight swallow but her eyes still flashed at him with glittering heat. 'You insulted me,' she said. 'You as good as called me a slut.'

'I want you, Lexi,' he said in a low, husky tone. 'And you want me. Deny it if you must but it's not going to go away.'

'It has already gone away,' she said, swallowing again.

'You want me,' he said again. 'Go on, admit it.'

'I will do no such thing!' she said, struggling to put some distance between their bodies. 'You just want me because you can't have me.'

'Oh, I can have you,' he drawled. 'Make no mistake about that, sweetheart. Engaged or not, I can have you and we both know it.'

She pushed away from him, glowering at him with venomous hatred as she wrenched open the door. 'You're wrong, Sam,' she said. 'You're so wrong.'

'Let's see about that, shall we?' he asked.

Lexi closed the door on his mocking smile, running, stumbling down the corridor as if the very devil himself was at her heels.

CHAPTER SIX

EVIE was coming back into the hospital as Lexi was leaving it. 'Hey, what's the rush?' Evie asked. 'You look like you're running from a fire.'

Lexi worked hard to get her flustered features under some semblance of control. 'I have a lot to get done,' she said. 'Things to do, people to see, you know.'

'Have you been to see Bella?' Evie asked.

'Um…no,' Lexi said, averting her gaze. 'I got distracted with…with, er, something else.'

Evie cocked her head. 'What's that on your face?'

'What's what?' Lexi asked, putting a hand up to her hot cheek.

Evie peered closer. 'It looks like some kind of rash…' She straightened and gave Lexi a narrow-eyed look. 'Beard rash. Where the heck would you get beard rash from when your fiancé is several thousand kilometres away, working in a remote Nigerian village?'

'Evie, don't,' Lexi said, releasing an impatient breath. 'I'm really not in the mood for this.'

'It's Sam Bailey, isn't it?' Evie said, frowning.

'Don't be ridiculous.'

'I saw you talking to him the other night at the pub. You were by yourselves for ages, looking all cosy in the corner. What's going on?'

Lexi threw her older sister a look. 'You're a fine one to talk,' she said. 'Everyone was talking about you and Finn that night. Finn was looking at you as if he wanted to strip you naked right then and there. Have you got something going on with him?'

Evie pulled her chin back in disgust. 'Are you crazy? I hate Finn's guts. You know that. He's the most arrogant, bull-headed man I've ever met. He probably left the pub with one of the barmaids. It wouldn't be the first time. That's the sort of jerk he is. Anyway, stop changing the subject. What's going on with you and Sam Bailey?'

'Nothing,' Lexi snapped irritably. 'Why does everyone assume there's something going on just because we were once involved? There's absolutely *nothing* going on. How many times do I have to say it?'

Evie looked at her for a lengthy moment. 'You *are* in love with Matthew, aren't you?' she asked.

'Of course I love him,' Lexi said. And she meant it. She really did. Matthew Brentwood was one of the nicest men she'd ever met. He treated her with respect; he made her feel important and special. It wasn't his fault she didn't enjoy being intimate with him. He hadn't done anything wrong. In fact, he had been incredibly patient with her. She hated herself for disappointing him. So many other men would have ended the relationship but, no, he had insisted it would get better once they were married. She felt safe and secure knowing he would always be there for her in spite of her shortcomings. She felt a treasured part of his loving family. His parents and two sisters had welcomed her with open arms. Her relationship with Matthew would never be a hair-raising, white-knuckle roller-coaster ride; it was more like a safe, gentle cruise on a peaceful lake.

It was what she wanted.

'Loving someone isn't the same as being in

love,' Evie said. 'Sometimes a relationship can feel right but be totally wrong.'

'There's nothing wrong with my relationship with Matthew,' Lexi said. 'I just wish people would mind their own business.'

'Sor-ry,' Evie said. 'No need to be so prickly.'

'I'm sorry,' Lexi said, her shoulders going down. 'I'm just dealing with some stuff right now.'

Evie frowned. 'What stuff?'

Lexi gave her sister a direct look. 'Did you know Dad had threatened to end Sam's career five years ago?'

Evie blew out a whooshing breath. 'I thought you might stumble across that sooner or later. I was hoping you wouldn't find out.'

'You knew about it and didn't *tell* me?' Lexi asked.

'I didn't find out about it until the other night at the pub,' Evie said. 'Finn thought it highly amusing to think of Dad trying to suck up to Sam. I asked him what the hell he meant and he told me he'd always suspected Dad had had something to do with Sam leaving. I had no idea he had pulled that sort of stunt. When we heard Sam had left, we all assumed he'd got some sort of scholarship to study overseas. Looking back now, I think Dad encouraged everyone to think that. He wouldn't have wanted anyone accusing him of blackmail.'

'No,' Lexi said bitterly. 'Instead, he made me think Sam had left because he couldn't care less about me. How could he do that? How could he act so despicably and think it wouldn't have consequences?'

'You can't change anything now, Lexi,' Evie said. 'You were so young back then. You wouldn't have stayed with Sam in the long term. Surely you realise that?'

'How do you *know* that?' Lexi asked with a furious glare. 'How can you be so sure of what I would or wouldn't have done?'

Evie frowned again. 'No need to bite my head off, Lexi.'

'I'm tired of everyone interfering,' Lexi said, clenching her hands into tight balls of tension. 'I'm so angry with Dad. I'm angry at Sam. But most of all I'm furiously angry at myself.'

'I don't see why,' Evie said reasonably. 'You

thought you were in love and got caught up in the fantasy of it. It's what kids do.'

'I was nineteen, not nine,' Lexi said. 'I was old enough to know my own mind. I should have fought for what I wanted. Why was I so weak? Why didn't I stand up for myself?'

'Lexi…' Evie's tone softened. 'Just let it go, OK? You're going to make yourself miserable in the long run. You can't live your life looking back over your shoulder all the time. You're happy and settled now. Don't go stirring up a hornet's nest just for the heck of it.'

'You don't understand,' Lexi said, fighting tears. 'Dad ruined my life. He's ruined everything.'

'I know it's hard for you to finally realise Dad isn't perfect,' Evie said. 'You've had him on a pedestal for such a long time. And while I don't agree with his methods, I think his motives probably came from the right place. He was worried about you wrecking your life. Sam was so much older and he was battle-scarred. Dad could probably see that and just did what he could to protect you.'

'I wish he'd left me to sort my own life out,' Lexi said bitterly. 'Why did he have to play God?'

'Tread carefully, Lexi,' Evie cautioned. 'You've got enough on your plate with organising the ball as well as your wedding without looking for more drama from home. You know what Dad's like. He can be an absolute bastard if you get on the wrong side of him. I should know. I've done it enough times.'

'I don't care,' Lexi said with a steely look of determination. 'I'm going to have it out with him. I don't care if he gets upset and rants and raves. I want him to face what he's done. He's coming back tonight from his weekend away. I can't just ignore this. I can't let him get away with it. It's my life, my happiness we're talking about here.'

Evie let out a sigh. 'You won't get him to apologise, Lexi. You do know that, don't you?'

Lexi set her mouth into an intractable line. 'I want him to realise you can't use people like chess pieces on a board. You just can't do that.'

'Good luck with it, hon,' Evie said. She paused

before she added, 'Oh, and maybe you should try a little concealer on that rash before you go home.'

Sam walked back to his office with the taste of Lexi still fresh on his tongue and the skin of his cheek still stinging from her slap. He knew he had probably deserved it. He had goaded her. He couldn't seem to stop himself from needling her. He had wanted a rise out of her. He had wanted her all stirred up and fiery. It made his blood thrum when she looked at him with those flashing sparks in her big blue eyes and her beautiful breasts heaving in anger.

He *had* wanted to kiss her. No point denying it. He had wanted to from the first day he'd run into her in the car park. She kept waving that flashy engagement ring under his nose but the way she'd kissed him back just now made him wonder if she was as in tune physically with her fiancé as she was with him.

And that was another thing there was no point denying, even though she seemed stubbornly determined to do so. Their physical chemistry was as strong and overpowering as ever.

He was going to have to watch his step. Having an illicit affair with Lexi now wouldn't be a great career move, not with her engaged to one of the hospital's biggest supporters. But, oh, how he wanted her! It was a constant ache in his flesh. He had only to think of her and he was swelling with need.

He was still having trouble processing the news of her virginity. How had he not noticed that? It made him feel uneasy that he had rushed her into bed without considering the implications. They had mostly practised safe sex. Mostly. He had only once…OK, maybe it had been twice… failed to use a condom in his haste to have her in the shower. His stomach clenched when he thought of how much he had demanded of her back then. She had met those demands with unbridled enthusiasm but it still made him feel he had exploited her. There was so much about Lexi he hadn't known back then. But now he suspected her sassy, smart-mouthed comebacks were a shield she hid behind when she was feeling threatened. She played the nose-in-the-air socialite role so well. The way she looked down her cute little nose at him, calling him country boy as if he still had hay between his teeth. Hell, it only made him want her more!

Maybe he was being overly cautious about the career risk. Maybe a short get-it-out-of-his-system affair would clear the air between them. After it was over—and he knew it would be over within a month at the most because he never played for keeps—he could move on with his life and she could go and marry her millionaire. Of course he knew it was wrong; of course if he were the fiancé and she was having an affair with someone else he wouldn't stand for it; of course it was madness. Sheer madness. But right now he wanted her too much to get tied up in moral knots over it.

Susanne was behind the reception desk when Sam came back in. 'There's an organ retrieval scheduled at Sydney Met at six this evening,' she said. 'The patient's family have decided to withdraw life support. He's a twenty-seven-year-old motorcycle victim who sustained severe head injuries three weeks ago. His kidneys are going to Perth, his heart to Melbourne and his lungs here.'

'Whose blood or tissues match have we got?' Sam asked.

'Mr Baker with the chronic obstructive airways disease,' Susanne said. 'He's been on the priority list the longest.'

'Right,' Sam said. 'You'd better call him and let him know. And organise theatre space. Things are going to get busy around here.'

Lexi was in the main lounge room at the family mansion in Mosman when her father finally walked in. She had been pacing the floor for the last hour, anger roiling inside her like a turbulent tide.

'Hello, beautiful,' Richard Lockheart said as he sauntered in. 'How was your weekend?'

Lexi folded her arms and shot him a glare. 'I've had better.'

Richard moved to the drinks cabinet and poured himself a Scotch. He lifted the lid on the ice bucket to find it was empty. 'Be a darling and get your poor old father some ice, will you?'

'I think you're perfectly capable of getting your own ice,' she said through stiff lips.

Richard smiled indulgently as he looked at her,

his dark brown eyes crinkling up at the corners. 'What's up, baby girl? That time of the month?'

Lexi suddenly realised how little she liked her father. Sure, she loved him, but she didn't much like him. Why had it taken her this long to see through his easy charm to the ruthlessly ambitious man beneath? If people got in the way of his plans he removed them. If people displeased him he made sure they lived to regret it.

She had always blamed her mother for deserting the family, but now she wondered if what Bella had said was right. Perhaps her father had had more to do with her mother leaving than anything else. She had heard rumours of his womanising behind her mother's back, but as a little girl she hadn't wanted to think of her father as anything other than blameless. It was a cruel shock to realise how she had been duped. How silly she had been to invest so much emotion and dedication in a parent who had callously used her for his own gain. Her whole life, both childhood and young adulthood, had been nothing but a house of cards that was now tumbling down around her feet.

'I found out about how you blackmailed Sam

Bailey five years ago,' she said. 'How could you do that? How could you play with people's lives in such a heartless way?'

Richard's brown eyes hardened. 'You don't know what you're talking about, Lexi.'

'I *do* know what I'm talking about,' she said. 'You issued an ultimatum to Sam. He had no choice but to leave. He could have lost his career, but did you care? No. All you wanted was to get him out of the way so you could keep me under your thumb. You didn't even have the guts to tell me he was being appointed here. I had to find out by myself. How do you think I felt?'

'You're in charge of fundraising,' he said. 'You have nothing to do with the hiring and firing of staff. Anyway, I'd assumed you'd forgotten all about him by now.'

Lexi clenched her hands so tightly her nails dug into her palms. 'Like you do with all of your lovers?' she asked. 'Just how many were there while you were married to Mum? Four? Five? Ten? Or have you *forgotten*?'

Her father's mouth tightened and he put his glass down with a loud thwack on the bar. 'What is all this nonsense, Lexi?' he asked. 'I don't expect to come home after a hard day at the office to this sort of behaviour.'

'You don't know what a hard day's work is,' she tossed back. 'You spend most of your time at boozy business lunches and resort weekends paid for by other people. Grandad did all the hard work. You just sit back and enjoy the benefits. You pay other people to do the dirty work for you, like bring up your children, for instance. You don't even take time out of your busy social schedule to visit Bella in hospital.'

Richard's face was almost puce in colour. 'I will not have you speak to me like this in my own house.'

'You told lies about me to Sam,' Lexi said, her anger rolling in her like a cannonball on a steep slope, and she couldn't have held it back if she tried. 'You told him I was only sleeping with him as part of some sort of teenage rebellion. How could you have done that?'

Richard thumped his hand down on the nearest surface so hard it made the pictures on the wall behind shake. 'You were too young to know your own mind. I did what I had to do to protect you.'

Lexi felt like screaming. The hurt inside her

was like a bottle of soda that had been shaken and was fit to explode. 'You had no right to interfere with my life,' she said. 'Not then and certainly not now.'

Richard gave her a disgusted look. 'I suppose he wants you back in his bed,' he said. 'Is that what this is about? You'd be a fool to jeopardise your engagement to Matthew. Sam Bailey will only use you to get where he wants to go. Don't ever forget that, Lexi. He's a boy from the bush who made good. A society bride like you would be the icing on the cake.'

'You have no idea how much damage you've done,' she said, too angry for tears.

'The only damage you should be worrying about right now is raising sufficient funds for the hospital,' Richard said with a sneer. 'Carrying on like a lovesick teenager while you're supposed to be concentrating on the ball is going to feed into people's doubts that you're not the right person for the job. I had to work hard to convince the board to agree to have you as Head of Events. If you stuff this up now, you'll not only be made a laughing stock but you'll make me look a fool as well.'

'I hardly think you need any help from me in making yourself look a fool,' she said. 'You do a pretty fine job of it all by yourself.'

Realising confrontation wasn't working, Richard put on the charm again. 'Now, now, baby girl,' he said. 'Aren't you being a little bit melodramatic? Forget about Sam Bailey. He's nothing to you now. You're happy with Matthew. He's perfect for you. You don't want to upset him and his family when they've been so supportive of the hospital, do you?'

Lexi glared at him. 'Why is everything always about money with you?'

'Money is a universal language, Lexi,' Richard said. 'It opens lots of doors and it shuts some others.'

Lexi turned and walked out of the room with her heart feeling as if someone had reached inside her chest and ripped it out. There were doors she could never open again. They were shut tight against her. She had been locked out of her own life by walking through the doors her father had opened for her.

But the most important door of them all she had slammed shut all by herself.

CHAPTER SEVEN

'WHAT do you mean, the venue's been cancelled?' Lexi looked at her assistant Jane in horror a few days later. 'The ball is in two weeks' time!'

Jane grimaced. 'I know,' she said. 'The manager wants to speak to you personally to apologise. He said there was a fire in the kitchen that got out of control last night. There's extensive water damage from the fire hoses. They're doing what they can to redecorate but they've had to cancel all bookings for the next month. Shall I get him on the line for you?'

Lexi nodded and took the call in her small office. It was as bad if not worse than Jane had described. After talking to the manager it was clear that the ball could not go ahead as planned. The kitchen was out of action, for one thing, and the ballroom was the worst hit in terms of water damage.

What a disaster!

Lexi felt as if everything she had worked so hard for had been ripped out from under her. She had put so much of herself into this job. She had invested a great deal emotionally in order to get her life back on track. Her father's cruel taunt came back to haunt her. It wasn't just her own lurking doubts about her ability to make a worthwhile contribution to society; it seemed everyone else felt the same. Everyone saw her as a shallow party girl with no substance. They didn't know half of what she had sacrificed to protect Bella. They didn't know how desperately she wanted to succeed. Bella's future—her life, everything—depended on Lexi getting the funds for the new equipment.

She *had* to prove them wrong. She had to show everyone, including herself, that she was up to the task no matter what last-minute hurdles were thrown at her.

She had to *think*.

She had to think past the thick fog of panic in her head and find a solution. What solution? All the tickets had been sold. The silent auction items were organised and confirmed. Everyone was looking forward to the big night of wining, dining and dancing and now it was not going to go ahead, not unless she could find another venue that could house that number of people at short notice. She spent an hour on the phone in the vain hope of finding a suitable venue but nothing was available. It was wedding season after all.

She pushed back her chair and went back to where Jane was sorting the silent auction placards.

'Any luck?' Jane asked hopefully.

Lexi shook her head in despair. 'Unless someone cancels their wedding at the last minute, I'm totally stuffed. Everyone's going to think it's my fault.'

'I'm sure no one will think that,' Jane consoled her.

Lexi gave her a grim look. 'Won't they?' She paced the floor in agitation. 'I can hear them now: "Lexi Lockheart only got the job because of her father and look at what a rubbish job she did of it."' She stopped pacing to grasp her head between her hands. 'Grr! I can't believe this is happening to me on top of everything else.'

'It's certainly a difficult time for you with Bella in hospital and your wedding so close,' Jane said in empathy.

Lexi stopped pacing and looked at Jane. 'That's it!' she said.

'What's it?' Jane asked, looking shocked. 'You're not thinking of cancelling *your* wedding, are you?'

'The hospital,' Lexi said excitedly. 'We'll have the ball here.'

Jane gaped at her. *'Here?'*

'Yes,' Lexi said, tapping her lips as she thought it through. 'The forecourt is big enough for a marquee. The patients can even be a part of it that way, those that aren't too ill, of course. We can get the caterers to do extra nibbles and desserts for all the patients on the wards. It'll be brilliant!'

'It sounds great but what will the CEO think?' Jane asked.

Lexi snatched up her purse and phone. 'I'll go and speak to him now. Wish me luck.'

'Good luck!' Jane called as Lexi dashed out of the door.

* * *

Sam looked up at the clock on the wall. 'Time of death: four-forty-six p.m.,' he said in a flat tone.

'You did your best, Sam,' the anaesthetist said over the body of Ken Baker. 'He'd been on the waiting list too long. He would've died anyway. He went into this knowing there was only the slimmest chance of success.'

Sam stripped off his gloves and threw them in the bin, his expression grim. 'I'll go and speak to the family,' he said, his stomach already in tight knots at the thought.

Losing patients was part of the job. Every surgeon knew it. Sam knew it but he still hated it. He hated the feeling of failure. Even when the odds were stacked against him he went into every operation intent on proving everyone wrong. And he had done it—numerous times. He had won some of the most unwinnable of battles. His professional reputation had been built on his successes. He had lengthened people's lives, given them back to their families, given them back their potential.

But this time he had failed.

And now he had to face the family and still act as if he was in control when he felt anything but.

The clinically composed veneer he wore was so thin at times he wondered why relatives didn't see through it.

The family was gathered in one of the relatives' rooms outside the theatre suites. Gloria Baker stood as soon as Sam came in. There was a son and a daughter with her, both teenagers about fourteen and sixteen. The son reminded Sam of himself at the same age: tall and awkward, both physically and socially. 'I have some very bad news for you,' Sam said gently. 'We did everything we could but he wasn't strong enough to survive the surgery. I'm very sorry.'

Gloria Baker's face crumpled. 'Oh, no…'

Megan, the daughter, wept in her mother's arms but the son, Damien, just sat there, expressionless and mute. Sam knew what that felt like. The inability to publicly express the devastation you felt inside. He could imagine what Damien was going through. How he would have to step up to the plate and support his mother and sister. Be the man of the house now his father had died. He would appear to cope outwardly and everyone would marvel at how brave he was being.

Sam had done the very same thing but inside he had felt as if a part of him had been lost for ever.

'I'm very sorry for your loss,' Sam said again.

'Can we see him?' Megan asked.

'Of course,' Sam said. 'I'll organise it for you. Take all the time you need.'

Gloria wiped at her eyes. 'Thank you for being so kind,' she said. 'Ken knew he might not make it. He's been sick for so long. I just wish you had been here earlier to help him.'

'I wish that too,' Sam said.

'You can come through now,' one of the scrub nurses said to the family.

Sam stood to one side as the Baker family walked into Theatre to say their final goodbyes. There were some days when he really hated his job. He hated the pain he witnessed, he hated the ravage of disease he couldn't fix, he hated the blood loss he couldn't control, he hated the long hours of tricky, delicate and intricate surgery that ended with a flat line on the heart monitor.

He let out a sigh and turned for the theatre change room.

He couldn't wait for this day to be over.

* * *

After a prolonged and difficult meeting with the hospital CEO Lexi had finally been given the go-ahead to restage the ball in the forecourt of the hospital. Her head was full of ideas for how the marquee would look. She still had a heap of things to do but she had already organised the layout and decorations. The caterers were booked and she had selected the menu. A wine supplier had donated several cases of wine and champagne and the hospital florist had offered her services for the table arrangements. Lexi had even sent out emails to all ticket holders on the change of venue and was now in the process of pinning flyers to all the staff noticeboards throughout the hospital. After that horrible panic when she'd first received the news it felt good to be back in control of things.

The lift opened on the doctors' room floor and Lexi stepped out with her bundle of flyers. She ran smack bang into Sam's broad chest and the sheaf of notices went flying. The air was knocked out of her lungs and all she could manage was a breathless 'Oops!'

Sam narrowed his eyes at her. 'Don't you ever look where you're going?' he snapped.

Lexi gave him an arch look. 'I thought you always used the stairs?'

His jaw clenched like a steel trap as he bent to retrieve the flyers. Lexi watched as his gaze ran over the announcement printed there. 'What's this?' he asked, swinging his nail-hard gaze to hers.

'It's a flyer about the ball,' she said, angling her body haughtily. 'There's been a change of plan.'

His dark brows met above his eyes in a frown. 'You're having the ball here? At the hospital?'

Lexi bent down to pick up the rest of the scattered bundle. 'Yes,' she said, tugging at one of the flyers beneath his large foot. She looked up at him. 'Do you mind?'

He stepped off it and she straightened, making a point of smoothing the flyer out as if it was a precious parchment he had deliberately soiled with his footprint.

'What happened to the other venue?' Sam asked.

'A fire in the kitchen,' Lexi said. 'The firemen went a bit overboard with the water. The place is a mess.'

Sam was still frowning. 'But surely this isn't the right place to have a function like that. Where are you going to house all the guests? The boardroom only fits twenty. That's going to put a whole new spin on dancing cheek to cheek. It'll be more like cheek to jowl.'

'I've organised a marquee,' she said with a toss of her head. 'It's all on the flyer if you'd take the time to read it.'

'Have you thought this through properly?' he asked. 'You're going to have people all over the place, some of them heavily inebriated. What about security? What about the disruption to the patients? This isn't a hotel. People are here because they're sick, some of them desperately so.'

Lexi rolled her eyes impatiently. 'I've already been through all this with the CEO. He's given me the all-clear.'

'A busy public hospital is not a party venue,' Sam said. 'It's a ridiculous idea. What were you thinking?'

Lexi was furious. She had only just managed to get the CEO on side. If Sam went up to him and expressed his concerns, the decision might very well be revoked. Her heart started to hammer in panic. She had to make this work. There was no other option. Her reputation was riding on this. She *had* to pull it off. 'Why are you being so obstructive about this?' she asked. 'Is it because I'm the one planning it? Is that it?'

'That has nothing to do with it,' he said with a brooding frown. 'I just don't think you've thought it through properly.'

Lexi glowered at him. 'Have *you* got a better idea, country boy? What about we throw a few hay bales around the local park and have a sausage sizzle and a few kegs of beer? Would you be more comfortable with that? Maybe we could even bring in some sheep and some cows for authenticity, or what about a pig or two? I bet that would make you feel right at home.'

Sam took her by the elbow and marched her out of the way of the interested glances coming their way. 'Will you keep your voice down, for heaven's sake?' he snarled.

She tugged at his hold but his fingers tightened. 'Get your hand off me,' she said. 'I'll call Security. I'll scream. I'll tell everyone you're harassing me. I'll… Hey, where are you taking me?'

Sam opened a storeroom door and dragged her in behind him, closing the door firmly once they were both inside. 'You want to pick a fight with me, young lady, then you do it in private, not out there where patients and their relatives can hear.'

'I suppose you think since you've got me all alone you can kiss me again.' She threw him a blistering glare. 'You just try it and see what happens.'

Sam gave her a taunting smile as he stepped closer. 'I can hardly wait.'

Her eyes rounded and she backed up against the storage cabinet, making it rattle slightly. 'Don't you dare!'

'What are you afraid of, Lexi?' he asked, picking up a strand of her hair and looping it around his fingers. 'That you might kiss me back and enjoy every wicked moment of it?'

He saw her slim throat rise and fall over a swallow and the way she sent the tip of her tongue out over her lips, a quick nervous dart that deposited a fine layer of glistening moisture on their soft pillowy surface. 'I'd rather die,' she said with a hoist of her chin and a flash of her bluer-than-blue eyes.

Sam knew he was not in the right mood to be rational. He knew he should have walked away from her and gone home and wrestled his demons to the ground the way he normally did. Take it out on the ocean where no one could see or hear. But being with Lexi even for a few stolen moments was what he wanted more than anything right now. He threaded his fingers through her hair, which felt like silk, fragrant silk that fell in a skein way past her shoulders. The blood was surging through his body, making him thick and heavy with want. She would feel it if he brought her any closer. Her feet had already bumped against his, her slim thighs just a hair's breadth away. 'Have you told your fiancé about us yet?' he asked.

Her eyes darkened like a thundercloud. 'No, why should I?' she said. 'There is no us. It's all in your head. You're imagining it. I don't even like you. I hate you, in fact. I can't think of a person I hate more. You're despicable, that's what you are. You think you can play games with people. You think you can make them do things they don't want to do. You want to make trouble. You want to mess up my life just when I've finally got it all…'

Sam brought his lips to the shell of her ear, trailing his tongue over the fragrant scent of her skin. 'Am I imagining this?' he asked.

He felt the expansion of her chest against his at her sharp intake of breath, her breasts brushing against him enticingly. 'Stop it,' she said in a whisper-soft voice but she didn't move away.

'And this?' he asked, stroking his tongue over the fullness of her bottom lip.

He felt her lips quiver as she snatched in another uneven breath. 'You shouldn't be doing this,' she said, her voice almost inaudible now. 'I shouldn't be doing this…'

'But you want to, don't you, Lexi?' he said, touching her mouth with his in a teasing brush of lips against lips. 'You want to so badly it's like a drug you know you shouldn't be craving but you can't control your need for it. It consumes you. It keeps you awake at night. Sometimes it's all you can think about during the day.' He teased her lips again, a little more pressure, lingering there a little bit longer until her breath mingled intimately with his. 'That's what it's like, isn't it, Lexi?'

Her eyelids came down, the long mascara-coated lashes screening the ocean-blue of her eyes. 'It's wrong...'

Sam cupped the nape of her neck. He felt her melt against him, like soft caramel under the heat of a flame. Her body meshed against his: her breasts to his chest; her slim hips to his achingly tight pelvis; her feminine mound brushing against the head of his erection, making him crazy with desire.

The sound of a mobile ringing from within the depths of Lexi's bag hanging off her shoulder fractured the moment.

'Are you going to get that?' Sam asked after several jarring peels of the ringtone.

She stepped away from him and fumbled in her bag to answer the phone. She looked at the screen before she answered, her cheeks going a deep shade of pink. 'Matthew...I...I was just going to call you.' She turned her back to Sam and continued, 'I miss you too… Yes…not long now…'

Sam let out a rough curse under his breath and, wrenching open the door stalked out, clipping it shut behind him.

Lexi checked both ways in the corridor before she left the storeroom. She patted her hair into place and walked briskly towards the medical ward to deliver the rest of the flyers as well as call in on Bella. She hoped Sam had already completed his rounds because she didn't want to run into him again, certainly not while she was still feeling so flustered. She had been so close to throwing herself into his arms. It had been a force so strong she had no idea what would have happened if Matthew hadn't called at that point.

Matthew.

Every time she thought of him the guilt was like a gnawing toothache. It just wouldn't go away. She would have to tell him about Sam, but how? How did you say to your loving and faithful fiancé that you were confused about your feelings for an ex? Their wedding was only a matter of weeks away. The dress was made. She had another fitting tomorrow. The invitations had long gone out and most of the RSVPs had been returned. Some people had even dropped in gifts, horrendously expensive ones too. How was she supposed to tell anyone, Matthew especially, that she was getting cold feet?

Lexi pulled herself back into line with a good mental shake. All brides got nervous before their big day. It was normal to have doubts. It was a big decision to get married. It was a huge commitment to promise to share your life with someone, to be faithful to them…

Her stomach flip-flopped as she thought of Sam's aroused body against her, and his mouth with its hot, sexy breath blending erotically with hers. She suppressed a forbidden shiver of delight when she thought about his tongue blazing a trail of fire over her sensitive skin. Her body was still aching from the hunger he had stirred in her. Would it always be this way? How was she going to navigate her way through her career and marriage to Matthew with Sam in the way?

She would be strong, that's how, she decided. She would garner her self-control.

She would be *determined*.

Bella was thankfully alone when Lexi entered the room. She was receiving oxygen through a nasal prongs tube and resting with her eyes closed, but she opened them as soon as she heard Lexi's footsteps.

'Hi, Lexi,' she said. 'I was wondering if you'd forgotten about me.'

'Sorry, Bells,' Lexi said. 'I've been run off my feet with the charity-ball arrangements. I suppose you heard what happened?'

'Yes, one of the nurses told me,' Bella said.

'It's all under control now…sort of,' Lexi said. She tidied up some fallen rose petals on the bedside chest of drawers. 'Is there anything I can get you? Do you want a proper coffee from the café? More magazines?'

Bella shook her head. 'No, I'm waiting for Mr Bailey to come in. I was in the shower when he came past this morning. He's been busy in Theatre most of the day. His first transplant case, or so one of the nurses said. Have you run into him lately?'

Lexi felt the heat rush to her cheeks and turned back to the flowers, willing some more petals to fall so she could keep her gaze averted. 'Not recently,' she lied.

The skin prickled along her arms as she heard the sound of voices out in the corridor. Sam was speaking to one of the nurses, ordering some bloods and scans for another patient. Lexi would recognise that deep, mellifluous voice anywhere.

'Are you OK, Lexi?' Bella asked.

Lexi painted a bright smile on her face as she turned around with the vase of flowers in her hands. 'I'm going to change the water on these flowers,' she said.

Bella frowned. 'But one of the volunteer ladies already did it this morning.'

'It won't hurt to do it again,' Lexi said. 'I might even get you some new ones from the hospital florist. These are just about past it.' She dashed out of the room and without even giving the nurses' station a glance slipped into the utilities room further down the corridor.

'Your oxygen levels have improved a bit, Bella,' Sam said as he read through her chart. 'The infection seems to have more or less cleared. I'd like you to stay in over the weekend just to make sure things have settled. If everything's fine you can go home on Monday, but you must take things easy. We'll have you on permanent standby in case a donor comes up. Has the transplant co-ordinator talked to you about the routine?'

Bella nodded. 'I have to have a mobile phone with me at all times in case there's a match, and a bag packed for the hospital.'

'Good.' Sam clipped the chart back on the end of the bed. 'Who will be looking after you at home?'

'Um…Lexi mostly,' she said.

Sam felt a frown tug at his forehead. 'You don't have a nurse to come in or a regular physiotherapist?'

'Yes, but Lexi's the one who takes me to all my appointments and helps me get dressed if I'm too breathless.'

Sam thought of Lexi juggling the demands of her job as well as the substantial care of her frail sister. It was another reminder to him of how she hid behind the shallow socialite facade when it suited her. But did she ever get noticed for the personal sacrifices she made? How could she if it drew attention to how much Bella relied on her? It would make Bella feel like an encumbrance, and he suspected that was something Lexi would want to avoid, given no one knew how long Bella would be with them. 'I'll have a word with the nurse about a follow-up appointment in my rooms,' he said. 'I'd like to keep a close eye on things just to be sure that infection doesn't come back.'

'Thank you, Mr Bailey,' Bella said shyly.

Sam gave her a brief smile and left to write up the last of his notes in the nurses' station. On his way out of the ward he ran into Evie, who was presumably on her way to visit Bella.

'Sam, can I have a quick word?' she asked.

'Sure,' he said. 'How about in here?' He gestured to a small waiting area that was currently empty.

'It's about my sister,' Evie began as soon as they were alone.

'I'm discharging her on Monday,' Sam said.

'Not that sister,' Evie said with a direct look. 'I meant Lexi.'

Sam drew in a measured breath. 'I see.'

'Actually, I don't think you do see,' Evie said,

shooting him a look. 'Lexi's in a good place right now. She's getting married in a matter of weeks. She doesn't need the complication of an ex turning up and distracting her.'

Sam raised an eyebrow. 'Distracting her?'

Evie narrowed her gaze at him. 'I think you know what I mean.'

'Lexi's an adult,' he said. 'She's entitled to do what she wants.'

Evie's hazel eyes were brittle as they stared into his. 'She doesn't know what she wants,' she said. 'That's half the problem.'

'Then she should be left to decide without the influence of others,' Sam said coolly.

'You don't understand,' she said. 'Lexi had a really rough time after you left. I was very worried about her. I'm sure she didn't tell me even half of what was going on. She didn't tell anyone.'

Sam felt something in his stomach turn over suddenly. 'What do you mean?'

Evie pulled at her bottom lip with her teeth before she answered. 'She was so...different after you left. She was flat, depressed even. She closed off from everybody. It was like a wall was around her. No one could get to her and she wouldn't allow anyone in. It's only been since she's been involved with Matthew that she's started to blossom again.'

'I'm not sure what this has to do with me,' Sam said.

Evie glared at him. 'It has *everything* to do with you. People are starting to talk about you both. They think something's going on between you two. Something serious.'

'Perhaps you've misheard the gossip,' he said. 'The rumours that are circulating are about you and Finn, not me and Lexi.'

A rosy flush stained Evie's cheeks. 'That's complete and utter rubbish!'

Sam cocked his eyebrow again. 'Is it?'

Evie folded her arms across her body, just like her baby sister did when she felt threatened, Sam noted. 'I saw Lexi's face the other day,' she said accusingly. 'She had beard rash.'

Sam kept his face blank. 'So?'

'So?' Evie fumed. 'You have no right to kiss her! She's engaged to another man.'

'I wouldn't kiss any woman who wasn't an active participant,' he said with deadly calm.

Evie's eyes flared with anger. 'So you're saying she actively encouraged you? That's an outright lie! She's not a slut, far from it. In fact, I suspect you were her first lover. Did you know that at the time? I bet that's why you targeted her. Quite a notch on your belt, wasn't it? The youngest Lockheart sister. What a trophy to flash around.'

Sam tightened his mouth. 'I think you should concentrate on your own life and let your sister get on with hers.'

'You're not good for her, Sam,' Evie said. 'You unsettle her. She deserves to be happy. She deserves someone who'll love her, not use her as a stepping stone to get where he wants to go.'

'Is that what you think this is about?' Sam asked, frowning.

'What else could it be?' she asked. 'You don't love her, do you? If you loved her you wouldn't have let anyone stop you from seeing her. You would've fought for her no matter what it cost you personally or professionally.'

Sam gritted his teeth until his jaw ached. 'I don't love anyone like that,' he said.

Evie gave him a pitying look. 'Then maybe you should learn.' And with that she was gone.

CHAPTER EIGHT

FOR the last couple of weeks Lexi had more or less managed to avoid any lengthy contact with her father. She had worked late and then gone to the gym in the evenings, barely exchanging more than a few desultory words with him before she went to bed at night or left for work in the morning. But on the weekend before the ball she knew it would be harder to keep out of his way unless she had a plan to keep away from the family mansion for most of the time.

She had a dress fitting in the city at ten and rather than drive and struggle with finding somewhere to park she decided to catch a ferry across the harbour. It was one of those perfect Sydney spring days: warm and sunny, with a light breeze with a smell of summer to it. The harbour was dotted with yachts making the most of the wonderful weekend weather. Lexi wondered if Sam was out there somewhere, carving through the sparkling water, but she didn't see any vessel called *Whispering Waves*, even though she looked long and hard.

After the fitting Lexi did a bit of shopping, more than a bit, she thought a little ruefully as she juggled the bags of lingerie, clothes, shoes and make-up in both hands as she made her way back to Circular Quay for the ferry late in the afternoon. Rather than go straight home she wandered for a while along the Neutral Bay marina, looking at the million-dollar yachts moored there. There were a couple of yachties about doing maintenance, the smell of fresh paint in the air. The distinctive clanging sound of the rigging knocking against the masts in the breeze made her think of how wonderful it would be to just hop on a boat and sail away into the sunset, away from all of life's complexities. She wondered if that was what Sam did to relax after complicated surgery. She could picture him standing at the helm, his strong, tanned arms hauling sails and spinnakers up and down, enjoying the challenge of conquering the powerful and sometimes unpredictable conditions.

At the far end of the marina Lexi saw a white

yacht with dark blue lines painted on the sides and in simple cursive the name *Whispering Waves*. There was no sign of anyone about so she walked closer. It was a beautiful vessel, not top-end luxury but close to it. It was at least forty feet long and well maintained, the paint-work looked fresh and the decks were varnished a rich jarrah red.

Lexi checked if anyone was watching before she climbed aboard, her shopping making the task a little more difficult for her, but somehow she managed to get on deck in one piece with all her shopping still safe. She had a quick look around; rationalising that it was her duty as Head of Events to ensure the yacht was suitable for a party of eight for lunch.

To her surprise the door to below deck was unlocked. She had a little battle with her con-science as she thought about having a quick peek around. It was trespassing, she knew that. But then she knew Sam. That kind of made a differ-ence, didn't it? Anyway, she'd only take a min-ute to two. He would never even know she had been on board.

She strained her ears for any sound below,

and once she was certain all was clear, she went down the steps to look inside. It was so much more spacious than she had imagined. There was a kitchen with all the latest appliances off the lounge and dining area. There was plenty of storage along the sides of the living area and a bar with a drinks fridge set in next to a sound system. There was a bathroom and toilet complete with shower and vanity. She opened another door and found the master bedroom with its own en suite. The bed was made up with white linen with a black trim, and black and white patterned scatter cushions were placed neatly in front of the large soft pillows.

Lexi was about to test the bed when she heard a footfall on the deck above. Her heart gave a little flutter as she considered her options.

Come out or hide.

How was she going to explain being in his bedroom? Why, oh, why hadn't she thought about the possibility of him returning? He had probably only stepped off the yacht for a few minutes. It was going to take quite some talking to get herself out of this sticky situation. She could just imagine the conclusions he would jump to. There was only one thing to do…

She chose to hide.

There was a row of tall cupboards on one side of the master bedroom. The first one she opened was filled with drawers that weren't big enough to hide her things so she quickly opened the next one. She stuffed her shopping bags below some of Sam's wet-weather gear, closing the door as softly as she could. Her heart was still galloping as she opened another closet. It had more hanging space and was just big enough for her to squeeze in amongst Sam's casual shirts. But while it was an excellent hiding place, she decided against closing the door completely as the lock was a one-way affair. While she wouldn't go as far as describing herself as claustrophobic, the thought of spending the next hour or two— or longer—locked inside a dark cupboard didn't hold much appeal, so instead she hooked the tip of her index finger around the edge to keep the door ajar.

Lexi heard Sam move about above deck. She pictured him doing maintenance like the other men she'd seen. Scrubbing the decks or fixing the stay ropes or some such thing. He probably wouldn't stay long. It was coming on for six p.m. He'd probably leave in a half an hour, tops. Maybe even fifteen minutes. Ten if there was someone watching over her.

Sam frowned as he released the mooring ropes. Did he really have it so bad that he could smell Lexi's perfume wherever he went? He breathed in again, deeper this time. No, he was imagining it. All he could smell was the briny ocean, which was exactly what he needed right now. This was where he could forget about yesterday's failure. He had the rest of the weekend to be alone out on the harbour, to sail, to fish, to think, to find that inner calm he badly needed right now.

He started the engine and motored out of the marina, giving a wave to one of the young lads who'd helped him rig up a new sail the other day.

He had just enough time before sundown to get to his favourite hideaway. He could already taste that first refreshing sip of beer.

OK. Lexi tried to talk herself out of panic when she felt the yacht moving away from the marina. He was probably just taking it out for a test run. That's what yacht owners did sometimes. They didn't always go out for the whole weekend. He would come back and she could slip away without him noticing. It'd be a piece of cake. He would never know he'd had a stowaway on board.

After a while she lost track of time. How far was he going for pity's sake? New Zealand? The Cook Islands? She was hungry, so hungry her stomach was making noises not unlike the growl of the yacht's engine.

Finally, after what seemed like hours, the movement stopped. There was the mechanical sound of an anchor being released and then silence all but for the gentle slip-slap of water and the mewling cry of a seagull passing overhead.

Lexi's finger was aching from being curled around the cupboard door for so long. Her need for the bathroom had long overtaken her need for food. She would have crossed her legs if there had been room.

Sam's footsteps sounded again, closer this time. Lexi held her breath, her heart beating so hard and fast it was like a roaring in her ears.

She heard the sound of clothes being removed, and then—heaven help her bladder—the sound of the shower running. After the longest three minutes of her life she heard Sam towel himself dry and then open the cupboard with the drawers inside.

Beads of perspiration were trickling between Lexi's breasts. Her breathing was now so ragged she felt like her lungs were going to collapse. She looked down at the sliver of light coming through the gap where her finger was keeping the door ajar. She very carefully and very slowly brought her finger out of sight, holding her breath as she closed the cupboard with a soft click. She fought against the panic of being locked in a confined space.

It was dark.

Very, very dark.

Another cupboard opened further along the wall and she heard the rustle of fabric and then a slide of a zipper. Lexi knew what was next. He had just put on his jeans, now he would come looking for a shirt. There was no point in cowering in the dark in the hope he wouldn't see her. Of course he would see her. She would have to brazen it out and think of a very good excuse, like in about two seconds flat, for why she was in his shirt cupboard.

Sam opened the cupboard door and reared back in shock, a swear word slipping out before he could stop it. 'What the freaking hell are you doing?' he asked.

Lexi stepped out of the cupboard with a yellow shirt in one hand and a blue one in the other. 'I'm thinking the blue,' she said, holding it up against his shoulder, her head tilted on one side musingly. 'It goes better with your eyes. Yellow is so not your colour. It washes you out. Makes you look anaemic.'

Sam was still trying to get his heart rate under control. He really wondered for a moment if he was suffering a hallucination. But, no, it was Lexi in the flesh all right, every gorgeous inch of her, on his boat, alone with him. A hint of devilry made his mouth kick up at the corners. She was alone with him for the rest of the weekend. 'I hope you've packed a toothbrush because I'm not turning back to take you home,' he said.

'You have to take me home,' she said dropping the shirts, her sassy facade slipping. 'You have to turn back right now. Right this instant. I had no idea you were planning to sail to Tahiti or wherever it is you've taken me.'

Sam gave a soft chuckle. 'Tahiti sounds nice,' he said. 'I've never been there—have you?'

Lexi pushed past him to the en suite. She turned and glared at him before she went in. 'Do you mind giving me a little privacy?'

He folded his arms across his naked chest, jeans-clad legs slightly apart. 'Don't mind me,' he said. 'I've heard it all before.'

She narrowed her eyes to paper-thin slits. 'I hate you, do you realise that? I positively loathe you.'

'Probably a good thing considering you're engaged to someone else and we're stuck on this boat together until tomorrow evening at sundown,' he said.

Lexi's eyes went wide in horror. 'You're *kidnapping* me?'

'I'm not asking for a ransom so, no, I'm not kidnapping you,' he said. 'You invited yourself on board so you'll have to obey the captain. That's me, if you haven't already figured it out.'

Lexi flung herself into the en suite and snapped

the lock into place. She wanted to drum her fists on the door and scream like a banshee. If anyone found out she was on Sam's yacht for the weekend her life would be over. She would never live it down. The gossip would be unbearable.

No one needs to find out.

The traitorous thought slipped into her mind like a curl of smoke under a door. She had her mobile phone with her. She could text her sisters to say she was away for the weekend with a friend. She didn't have to say which friend. She didn't have to say it was her worst enemy. Hopefully they wouldn't put two and two together. Evie and Bella both knew she was trying to keep her distance from their father. They would assume she was staying out of town or something to avoid him.

Lexi came out of the en suite to find Sam had gone on deck. She made her way up to the bridge where he was standing looking towards the west, where the sun was sinking. The sky was a rich palette of red and ochre and gold. A flock of fruit bats flew past on their way to feed on the native trees and shrubs of the bushland on the shore about fifty metres away. It was a picturesque spot and the tranquillity after the hectic pace of the city earlier was not lost on Lexi. She breathed in deep, salty breaths and the scent of eucalypts that had spent all day being warmed by the sun.

Sam turned to look at her. 'Would you like a drink?' he asked.

Lexi folded her arms crossly. 'I suppose you always keep champagne on ice in case you get lucky.'

His eyes smouldered as they held hers. 'Always.'

Lexi glared at him defensively. 'I was doing an inspection. I happened to be in the area and saw your boat so I decided to have a look around.'

'Did it pass muster?' he asked with a teasing glint, 'or do you think the closet is too small?'

She tightened her mouth. 'You could definitely do with some more hanging space.'

He bent to pick up a loose rope, coiling it expertly in his hands as he continued to look at her. 'I think we both know you weren't really doing an inspection,' he said. 'You must have known I was about. The boat wasn't locked up. You were having a little snoop and then you heard me come back on board so you went into hiding.'

She threw him a petulant look. 'I wasn't *hiding*.'

He elevated one dark eyebrow. 'What were you doing?' he asked. 'Colour co-ordinating my shirts?'

Lexi brushed some hair back off her too-hot face. 'It was a knee-jerk reaction,' she said. 'I didn't know who was coming. It might have been a robber or a vandal or…or something…'

'Or a kidnapper.' A lazy smile played around the corners of his mouth.

Lexi bit her lip. 'Did you mean it when you said you won't take me back home until tomorrow evening?'

He stepped over a guy rope and came to stand closer to her. 'This is the first free weekend I've had in months,' he said. 'I wanted to spend it out on the water. Commune with nature. Relax, chill, unwind.'

'I'm sure you'd much rather be alone so if you just set me off somewhere I'll catch a cab back,' Lexi said.

Sam laughed. 'You see any cabs along this part of the coast?' he asked.

Lexi looked at the coastal reserve that fringed

the shore for miles along the headland, and frowned. She swung her gaze back to Sam's amused one. 'You have no right to keep me here against my will. I bet you're doing this on purpose to ruin my reputation. That's what this is about, isn't it?'

'No,' he said, taking her by the upper arms and bringing her flush against his rock-hard chest. 'This is what it's about.' And then he covered her mouth with the blazing fire of his.

It was an earth-moving kiss. Lexi felt her legs weaken like overcooked spaghetti as his mouth crushed hers in a deeply passionate assault on her senses. His tongue was a sensual sword that divided her lips to receive him. There was no denying him access. She had no willpower. No self-control. No determination. All she had was red-hot need. So hot it was burning from the soles of her feet, running up her legs, racing up her spine like a flame following a pathway of spilt gasoline. His tongue tangled with hers, teasing it into a sexy dance, taming it with the commanding thrust of his. She whimpered against his lips, her need for him so consuming she was almost sobbing with it. Her feminine folds were heavy with longing, the walls of her womanhood moist with the heat of hungry, rapacious desire.

Sam's grizzled jaw grazed the soft skin around her mouth as he shifted position. He cupped her face with his hands, his tongue snaking around hers in an erotic tangle that sent a rush of heat over her skin.

'I want you so badly,' he said against her swollen lips. 'I've never wanted anyone more than I want you right now.'

Lexi could feel the potent power of his erection against her belly. She could feel her body responding to his just as it had in the past. There was no need for words even if she could have found her voice. She let her body communicate all the pent-up longing she felt. She pushed herself against him, her breasts tight and sensitive, and her feminine mound contracting with a pulse of longing so strong she felt her legs sway beneath her.

Sam's hands gripped her hips, holding her against him, the friction of his arousal a torment to her senses. She welcomed the heat of him, rubbing against him shamelessly to assuage the ache that consumed her.

He slipped a warm hand beneath her top, pushing her bra aside to tease her nipple with the broad pad of his thumb. It was exquisite torture to feel him reclaim her flesh with the blistering heat of his touch. She gave a soft cry as he replaced his thumb with his mouth, his tongue swirling and stroking before he sucked on her with just the right amount of pressure.

She threw back her head in wanton abandon, arching her spine to give him greater access to her breasts. He moved from one breast to the other and back again, ramping up her desire until it was an all-consuming wave that threatened to sweep her away completely.

Lexi placed her hands on his chest, her mouth teasing his with little kittenish bites. Right now she was not the Lexi who was engaged to Matthew Brentwood. She had turned into a wild tigress of a woman eager to mate with her alpha male. Her body was Sam's and Sam's alone. It responded to his with a fervour that was unmatched by anything else in her experience.

Sam's mouth took control of the kiss, one of

his hands in the small of her back while the other worked on removing the rest of her clothes. Lexi stepped away from the soft pile of her garments, her mouth still locked on the fire of his. She felt the warm brush of his fingers against the hot wet heart of her. Her flesh was so responsive she knew it was too late to call an end to this madness. She felt the overwhelming pull of release deep within her body, all the nerves singing along the tight wires of her muscles as every sensation gathered to that one intimate point. One more stroke of his fingers and she plunged into the abyss, her body shaking with the tremors that rolled through her like the waves against the shore.

Sam held her as she came back from paradise but she could see his body was in urgent need of its own release.

'Condom,' he groaned against her mouth. 'I need to get a condom.'

Lexi was momentarily jolted out of the sensory spell. She suddenly felt the enormity of what she was doing. Sex was not just about physical needs being satisfied, or at least it wasn't for her. Her hands stalled in their exploration of his chest, her gaze lowered, her teeth sinking into her lip.

Sam lifted her chin to lock her gaze with his. 'You're not comfortable with taking this any further?' he asked. 'We don't have to. I understand. I really do.'

Lexi looked into the darkness of his desire-lit eyes and felt herself drowning. 'It's been such a long time,' she said. 'I'm not sure I can satisfy you the way I did before...'

He brushed her mouth with his, softly. 'Tell me to stop and I'll stop,' he said.

She cupped his face with her hands, her eyes dropping to his mouth. 'I don't want you to stop,' she said, surprised at how much she meant it.

He carried her below deck to his bedroom, placing her gently on the mattress. He looked down at her as she covered herself with her hands, as if she was embarrassed at being naked in front of him. 'You still OK with this?' he asked.

'Don't mind me,' she said. 'I'm just having a fat day.'

Sam smiled. That was what he loved about Lexi, the way she said the opposite of what he was expecting. He reached for a condom and applied it before joining her on the bed. He anchored his weight on his forearms, careful not to crush her. He couldn't help thinking of the first time he had made love to her. It had been rough and fast, over within seconds for both of them. He had hurt her. She had reluctantly admitted that. It tormented him to think he had done that to her. He should have prepared her young body with gentle handling, making sure her tender flesh could accommodate him. He would make up for it this time. He would worship her body the way he should have done the first time.

He started by kissing her mouth in a soft caress that gradually deepened. Her tongue met his and danced with it in a rhythm that was as old as time, a sacred rhythm that spoke of human connection at its most elemental.

Something shifted in his chest as he felt her arms come up around his neck, her fingers delving into his hair as her soft mouth responded to the gentle pressure of his. It was like a slip of a gear, a stumble of the heart that he hadn't been expecting.

She grew impatient beneath him, lifting her

slim hips, searching for him. Sam worked hard to control his urge to fill her. He had never had a problem with anyone else. Control came easily to him, but not with Lexi. He felt the magnetic pull of her core. He smelt the feminine fragrance of her, the sexy salt and musk that stirred his senses into overload.

He went back to her breasts with his mouth, teasing her with his lips and tongue until she whimpered and clawed at him. He continued down her body, dipping his tongue in the shallow cave of her belly button before going to her feminine folds. She was wet and swollen, like a precious hothouse flower, fragrant and heady, luscious and exotic.

He teased her apart with his tongue, taking his time, delighting in the cries she tried to suppress, relishing the way her back lifted off the bed as she convulsed.

Sam watched as her breasts rose and fell as she came back down to earth, her blue eyes looking almost shocked at how she had responded. He kissed her inner thigh and worked his way back up her body, taking his time, making sure she was ready for him to possess her.

'Please…' Her voice was a thready sound, an edge of desperation in it. 'Oh, Sam, *please…*'

Sam positioned himself, intending to string out the pleasure a little longer, but Lexi clearly had other ideas. She lifted her hips and he suddenly had nowhere to go but inside her. He surged in with a deep groan of pleasure as her tight body gripped him. He felt the ripples of her flesh, the intimate grasp of her massaging him until he was hovering on the precipitous edge of his control. He increased his pace, delighting in her slippery warmth as she wrapped her legs around his hips. Her supple body thrilled him, the way she had no inhibitions, the way she was so generous with her touch and caresses. Her mouth was soft but demanding, her tongue teasing and playful as it tangoed with his. He was getting closer and closer to the point of no return. It was a force building within him that was so powerful he could feel it roaring through his veins like a bullet train.

He pulled back from the brink to caress her with his fingers, to make sure she was with him when he finally fell. She gasped out loud as he played with her. He knew her body like he knew his own. He knew exactly what pressure and pace she liked, what she needed in order to be fulfilled. He felt the moment when she lost control; he felt the tight spasm of her body around him, milking him of his essence. He lost himself in her, falling, falling, falling into that blessed whirlpool of absolute, ultimate pleasure.

Sam held her close in the aftermath. He listened to the sound of her breathing slowly coming back to normal. For a moment it was easy to forget why he shouldn't have been lying with her breasts crushed against his chest and her legs still hooked around his hips.

'Oh, God,' she said.

Sam propped himself up on his elbows to look at her. 'Was that an "Oh God, I just had amazing sex" or an "Oh God, what have I done?"'

Her teeth pulled at her lip in that engaging way of hers. 'Both...'

He brushed the damp hair off her face with one of his hands. 'It was always going to happen, Lexi,' he said. 'I think we both knew that in the car park that day.'

She rolled out from under him and got off the bed. Her hair was all mussed up and her lips swollen from kissing. She took one of his shirts out of the closet and slipped it over her nakedness. His shirt was too big for her but Sam thought it looked far sexier on her than any lacy negligee.

He dealt with the condom before he went to where she was standing, grasping the edges of his shirt together to cover her body. He touched her on the cheek with one of his fingers. 'Hey,' he said. 'You don't have to hide yourself from me, Lexi. I know everything there is to know about your body.'

She gave him an agonised look. 'You don't… not really…'

He frowned as he looked at her. 'What do you mean?'

'Sam, I feel…I feel so guilty…'

He tipped up her chin with the same finger. 'It was just as much my fault as yours,' he said. 'I should've turned around once I found you on board and then none of this would've happened.'

She pulled his hand down from her face, stepping away from him, her arms wrapping tightly across her body again. 'I'm not talking about just now,' she said.

Sam frowned as he brought her back to face him with his hands on the tops of her shoulders. 'What *are* you talking about?' he asked.

He saw her throat go up and down and her eyes watered up, glistening with tears that threatened to fall any second. She bit her lip again, but still it trembled. Her whole body began to shake as if gripped by a fever.

'Sweetheart, what's wrong?' he asked, holding her steady with his hands on her upper arms.

She looked into his eyes for a long moment. 'Sam…I had a termination,' she said in a broken whisper. 'I had an abortion.'

He looked at her in a dumb silence. It took at least thirty seconds for him to process her words.

An abortion.

Which meant she had been pregnant at some point.

He said the first thing that came into his head. 'Was it mine?'

She turned away as if he had struck her. 'So that's the most important thing for you to establish, is it?' she asked.

Sam was having trouble keeping a lid on his

emotions. Lexi had been pregnant. She had been carrying *his* child. He had never envisaged himself as a father. It had always been in the too-hard, too-emotionally-challenging basket. And yet for a brief time, a few weeks, he had been a father, or at least a potential one. 'I'm sorry,' he said. 'That was unforgiveable of me. I wasn't thinking. Of course it was mine.'

'I didn't know what to do,' she said, still not looking at him. 'I was so frightened and alone. I went to your flat but you'd gone. I didn't know who to turn to.'

Sam thought of how it must have been for her, so young, so inexperienced and yet pretending to be so street smart. Her father wouldn't have been much use, or her mother. What else could she have done?

And yet…

He had almost been a father.

He thought of how it would be to have a son or daughter, a combination of their genes. What would their child have been like? His mind raced with images of a platinum-blonde little girl or a light brown haired little boy. Little arms and legs, fingers and toes, soft wispy hair…

'I'm sorry,' he said bringing himself back to the moment with an effort. 'I know it's not enough but I'm truly sorry you had to go through that.'

She looked at him then, her gaze accusatory, incisive. 'You're angry,' she said. 'You think I did the wrong thing. Go on, say it. I can handle it. You think I did the wrong thing.'

Sam felt ambushed by emotion. He wasn't used to dealing with this bombardment of feeling. 'What do you expect me to say?' he asked. 'Congratulations on your abortion? For God's sake, Lexi, I might act all cool and controlled most of the time but you've just laid a whammy on me so you're going have to allow me a minute or two to process it.'

Her eyes were glistening with tears as she glared at him. 'Do you think it was easy to make that decision? I *agonised* over it. I cried and cried for what might have been, for what I wanted. But in the end I felt I had no choice but to do what I did. Do I think I did the right thing? Yes. Do I think I did the wrong thing? Yes. It was both the right and the wrong thing. Sometimes the hardest decisions in life are.'

'The decision to terminate a pregnancy is never an easy one,' Sam said. 'I don't believe any woman goes into it lightly. Even when it's clearly the right decision even on medical grounds it can take years if not a lifetime to resolve the guilt surrounding it. But if it's any comfort, I think you did the right thing, Lexi. You were far too young for that sort of responsibility. And, quite frankly, I'm not sure I would've been much help even if you had been able to tell me. I would've supported you, of course, but it would have been hard for both of us at that point in our lives.'

She let out a wobbly sigh. 'I'm so sorry…'

Sam stepped up to her and cupped her face. 'Don't be,' he said firmly. 'It's in the past. Let it stay there. You can't change it.'

'I'm glad I told you,' she said on another sigh. 'It's been so hard keeping it to myself for all this time.'

Sam frowned. 'You haven't told your fiancé?'

Her cheeks grew pink and her eyes moved away from his. 'I've wanted to…so often, but the time has never seemed right.'

'Lexi,' he said. 'You're marrying this guy in

a matter of weeks. You need to tell him everything.'

She flashed him a glare over her shoulder. 'Like what happened here just now?' she said. 'You think I should tell him I had ex sex because I was feeling a bit lonely?'

Sam clenched his jaw. 'Is that what you think?' he asked. 'You were feeling a bit lonely so you jumped into bed with me? Lexi, you know that's not what happened. We had sex because we can't keep our hands off each other. It has nothing to do with loneliness, yours or mine.'

She turned away, her body hunched as if she wanted to curl up and hide. 'I can't imagine you'd ever be lonely,' she said. 'You probably have heaps of women flocking after you wherever you go.'

'I've had relationships,' Sam said. 'Nothing serious and nothing lasting. I guess I'm not built that way.'

She turned and looked at him. 'So you're not thinking of marrying and having a family someday?'

Sam shook his head. 'Not my scene, I'm afraid. With a fifty per cent divorce rate I don't like my chances of getting it right. I don't want to screw up someone else's life as well as my own.'

'But your parents were happy, weren't they?' she asked.

Sam thought of his father and mother and how his mother's chronic illness had had such an impact on their relationship. How his father had limped along for the last twenty years, half alive, isolated with grief and guilt. 'Yes, but their relationship was one of those once-in-a-lifetime ones,' he said. 'Not everyone can achieve that. It's not realistic to expect there's someone out there who will meet all of your physical and emotional needs. And speaking of physical needs, is that your stomach I can hear growling with hunger?'

She put her hand over her stomach. 'You can hear that?'

'No, but I'm starving and I figured you might be too after all that exercise.'

Her face coloured up again. 'Why does being here with you feel so right but wrong as well?' she asked in soft voice.

Sam brushed her cheek with his finger. 'I think what you said a minute ago is very true.

Sometimes some of life's hardest decisions are both right and wrong at the same time. Let's just say this is right for now and leave it at that.'

CHAPTER NINE

LEXI had a shower while Sam made dinner. She tried not to think about the moral implications of spending the rest of the weekend with him on his boat. It was as if she had stepped into a parallel universe, one where she and Sam were able to be together, enjoying each other's company, taking things as they came rather than planning too far ahead.

She looked at her engagement ring and felt like she was looking at someone else's hand. She grappled with her conscience before she tugged the diamond off. She had to use some soap to remove it. Was that a sign of some sort? she wondered. She looked at the pale circle of skin where the ring had hidden her flesh from the sun. She knew she would have to talk to Matthew. But she wasn't prepared to do it via email or over the phone. She needed to see him face to face to explain…

To explain what exactly? That she was in love with another man?

Lexi let out a sigh as she reached for a towel. There was only one man she could ever love and that was Sam. She loved him with her heart. She loved him with her mind. She loved him with her body. She felt like her life was incomplete without him in it. Being without him was like only wearing one shoe. Her life felt out of balance. The love she felt for him was the love his parents had felt for each other. A love Sam didn't feel for her. He had made that pretty clear. His relationships were 'nothing serious and nothing lasting'. That included her. What he was offering her was casual and temporary, a weekend of sensual delight, but then what? He would go back to his life and she would go back to hers.

Maybe she wouldn't have to tell Matthew. Maybe she could just let this weekend be her attempt at closure and leave it at that. She would move on with her life, get married and have babies and build a future with a man who loved her, instead of pining after a man who didn't and never would.

Lexi dressed in one of the new outfits she'd

bought that day: a white halter-neck top and slim-fitting taupe pants. She bundled her damp hair up in a knot on top of her head, sprayed her wrists with the perfume she carried in her bag, and applied a light layer of lip gloss before joining Sam in the kitchen dining area.

'That smells delicious,' she said, sniffing the air appreciatively.

Sam turned from the pot he was stirring and handed her a glass of wine he had poured. 'Here you go,' he said. 'Dinner won't be long.'

Lexi took the wine and angled her head to see what he was cooking. 'What are you making?' she asked.

'Mediterranean fish casserole,' he said. 'One of my colleagues in the States is married to a chef. She took me on as a project and taught me to cook a little more than the meat-and-three-veg routine I'd grown up with.'

'You obviously enjoy it,' she said.

'Yes, I find it relaxing,' he said, putting the wooden spoon on the counter. 'What about you? Do you cook or leave it to the servants?'

Lexi slipped back into socialite mode. 'Of course,' she said airily. 'Why do something so menial when you can pay someone else to do it and clean up afterwards too?'

'What if you run out of money one day?' he asked.

'As if that's going to happen,' she said. 'I'm marrying a rich man, remember?'

Lexi watched as he turned back to stirring the pot, the line of his back and shoulders now tense. She wished now she hadn't goaded him. The atmosphere had changed to one of enmity and stiffness when before he had been so tender with her over the termination. 'Can I help with anything?' she asked.

'It's cool,' he said. 'I've got it all under control.' He turned and leaned back against the counter to look at her, his eyes running over her in appraisal. 'You look particularly beautiful,' he said. 'That wasn't what you were wearing before.'

'Lucky I did some shopping today,' Lexi said. 'Otherwise I would've had to go naked.'

His eyes smouldered darkly. 'Suits me.'

'I bought just about everything else but I didn't buy a toothbrush,' she said. 'I don't suppose you happen to have a spare?'

'I always keep a supply of basic necessities on board.'

Lexi gave him a cynical look. 'In case you get lucky.'

His mouth tilted in a sexy smile. 'I guess you could say today's been my lucky day.'

Lexi frowned and averted her gaze. 'Sam…'

One of his hands came down on her bare shoulder, the other touching her beneath her chin and forcing her gaze back to his. His eyes were dark and serious. 'If you really want to go back, I'll take you back,' he said.

Lexi didn't want to go back. She didn't ever want to go back. She wanted to stay on his boat with him for ever without the intrusion of other people telling her what she should and shouldn't do. 'No,' she said in a whisper-soft voice. 'I don't want to go back just yet.'

He brushed her forehead with a kiss before he stepped away to go back to his cooking. 'Good, because I've had a hell of a week and I really need to clear my head.'

Lexi watched as he went back to the simmering pot. He was frowning as he stirred the casserole, the set to his mouth almost grim. 'You want to talk about it?' she asked.

One of his shoulders went up and down. 'It's OK. I deal with this stuff all the time—patients dying on the table because they're too sick to survive the surgery. It's part of the job. You win some. You lose some. But I hate losing. I never get used to it.'

Lexi put her glass down and moved to stand behind him. She wrapped her arms around his waist and pressed her cheek to the hard wall of his back. 'I'm sorry,' she said softly. 'It must be so hard for you. No one thinks of how the surgeon feels. Everyone feels sorry for the patient and the relatives, but what about the surgeon who has to try to sleep at night haunted by all those people he wasn't able to save in time? It must be absolute agony for you.'

He turned in the loop of her arms and brushed a wisp of hair off her forehead with a gentle finger. 'We're supposed to get hardened by it during our training,' he said. 'I'm usually good at keeping my emotions separate. I have to, otherwise it can cloud my judgement. But I lost a patient yesterday. I guess that's why I bawled you out about the change of venue for the ball. I was in a foul mood. I'd just left a family to say goodbye to their husband and father in Theatre. He died during the procedure.'

Lexi looked up at him in distress. 'Oh, Sam, and I was such a cow to you.'

He gave her a rueful smile. 'I probably deserved it. I seem to always be baiting you. I guess I like getting a rise out of you. You're so adorable when you're spitting chips at me.'

Lexi gave him a sheepish look. 'I didn't mean it about the hay bales and farm animals…especially the pigs. That was a bit low.'

He grinned at her and walked her back against the table with his thighs against hers. 'Yes, you did, you little minx,' he growled playfully.

Lexi shivered as his lips found her neck, nipping at the skin in little bites that sent electric shocks throughout her body. He finally came to her mouth, sealing it with a kiss that made every nerve tingle with delight.

'I thought we were going to have dinner,' she said somewhat breathlessly.

'Later,' he said.

Lexi closed her eyes as she gave herself up

to his kiss. It was tender and searching, as if he was looking for the young innocent girl she had been, as if he was trying to redress the past by retracing his steps, doing things differently this time. She kissed him back with equal tenderness, enjoying the new-found intimacy that was so much more than two grappling bodies intent on sensual pleasure but more of a meeting of two spirits who found something special and priceless only with each other.

Sam finally eased his mouth off hers and brushed her hair back from her forehead, giving her a bemused smile. 'You constantly surprise me, Lexi Lockheart, do you know that?'

Lexi gave him a shy smile in return. 'Oh, I'm full of surprises, that's for sure.'

He reached for her ring hand, looking down at it before he met her eyes. 'Where's your engagement ring?' he asked.

Lexi couldn't read his masked expression. 'I…I took it off.'

'I don't suppose you tossed it overboard.'

She pulled her hand out of his and stepped away from him. 'Is that what you'd like me to do?' she asked.

He looked at her for a long moment. 'What *are* you going to do?'

Lexi bit her lip. 'I'm not sure…'

'Seems pretty simple and straightforward to me,' Sam said.

'Oh, really?' she said.

'Yeah,' he said. 'You shouldn't be marrying a man who doesn't satisfy you.'

Lexi put her hands on her hips. 'How do you know he doesn't satisfy me?'

He gave a shrug of one shoulder as if he didn't care either way. 'I figure if you were getting what you need from him, you wouldn't be here with me.'

'Maybe I need more than he can give me,' she said. 'You said it yourself. It's hard to find someone who meets all of your physical and emotional needs.'

'Do you love him?' Sam asked.

Lexi let out a snort of derision. 'Who are you to ask me about love?' she said. 'You don't love anything but your career.'

'Do you love him?' He repeated the question, more forcefully this time, which put her back up.

'Of course I love him!' She almost shouted the words.

'And yet you've told him nothing about what happened between us five years ago.'

Lexi glared at him. 'It's in the past. It should stay there.'

'I beg to differ, sweetheart,' he said. 'What's happened over the last couple of hours suggests it's not staying in the past. It's spilling into the here and now and at some point you're going to have to deal with it. You have to tell him.'

She gave him a cutting look. 'What do you want me to say to him? Do you want me to tell him you seduced me when I was barely out of school?'

His brows clamped together in a brooding frown. 'Don't go pulling that card on me, young lady,' he growled. 'You lied to me about your age. I wouldn't have touched you if you hadn't thrown yourself at me like a ten-dollar whore.'

Lexi raised her hand but he intercepted it mid-air, his fingers so tight, so cruelly tight she felt tears smart in her eyes. 'Let go of me, you bastard!'

'Stop it,' he said in a gritty, deadly calm voice. 'Get control of yourself.'

Lexi flew at him in a rage so intense she even frightened herself. She wanted to hurt him. She wanted him to have physical scars similar to the deep, painful emotional ones she had carried for so long. She fought him, tooth and nail, kicking at him, screaming words of abuse she had never used on anyone before.

But it was all in vain because he was too strong, too determined, too in control.

He held her until the fight went out of her. She went limp in his arms, her energy gone as if someone had pulled out the power source from her body.

She started to cry. Not soft little sobs but great big hulking ones that ripped at her chest like a pair of metallic claws. Tears rolled down her face but she could do nothing to stop them as Sam was still holding her in an iron grip.

But finally he relaxed his hold and the fingers that had bitten into her flesh began to stroke and soothe her instead. 'Hey,' he said softly.

'Don't you "hey" me,' she said, but not with any venom. She was way past that.

Sam drew her close against his body, his arms wrapping around her, his body moving from side to side in a soothing rocking motion, similar to one a loving mother did to a distressed child, not that Lexi had much memory of that experience, but she missed it all the same. 'Shh,' he said gently. 'No more tears, OK? I'm sorry. I didn't mean it. You didn't throw yourself at me.'

Lexi nestled against his strength and solid warmth. 'I did,' she mumbled against his chest. 'I acted like a tart. I'm so ashamed of myself. I don't know what came over me.'

She felt his hand stroke the back of her head, holding it close to his body. 'I could've walked away,' he said. 'I should've walked away.'

Lexi lifted her head off his chest to look at him. 'Why didn't you?'

His eyes were dark and warm, like melted chocolate. 'The same reason I didn't turn this boat around when I found you in my cupboard,' he said. 'I wanted you.'

Lexi felt her heart slip sideways in her chest. He wanted her, but for how long? Should she ask him? Would he put a time line on it? Or should she just take what was on offer and leave everything else to fate? 'I need to freshen up,' she said, lowering her gaze in case he saw the longing in hers.

He gave her a pat on the bottom. 'Take your time,' he said. 'I can hold dinner.'

The night sky was amazing as they sat out on the deck after they had eaten. Sam glanced at Lexi, looking as beautiful as ever though she was wearing one of his warm fleece jackets that swamped her slim frame. The wind had picked up, bringing with it a chill that was a reminder that the long lazy days of summer were still a few weeks away.

So too was Lexi's wedding, he thought with a clench of his gut. She may have taken her ring off but she seemed just as determined as ever to go ahead with the marriage.

He wasn't sure how he was going to deal with that day in November. It wasn't as if he would be invited. He wouldn't accept if he was. What he couldn't understand was why she would still want to marry someone who clearly wasn't meeting her needs.

He hated to think of her marrying for money.

It didn't fit well with the Lexi he knew now. The Lexi who put her sister's health and happiness above any of her own needs or desires, the Lexi who worked so tirelessly for the benefit of the hospital charity.

But, then, people married for a host of different reasons: companionship; security; common goals...*children.*

Sam thought back to when he had seen himself following in the footsteps of his father and grandfather and great-grandfather before him. Being a husband, then becoming a father, raising a family, providing for them. In the days before his mother had become so desperately ill he had thought about building a life with someone, having a brood of kids. It had seemed the normal thing to do. But then his mother had got sick and he had watched as his father had struggled to juggle everything: the farm and finances; Sam's needs; and those of his mother. It had broken his father, made him half the man he had been. His strong, tall, capable father had seemed to diminish and age right in front of Sam's eyes. It had terrified Sam to think that might one day happen to him.

Lexi was looking up at the sky. 'I think I can see a satellite,' she said.

'Where?' Sam said, joining her on the cushioned seat at the stern.

She pointed to a moving light in the black velvet of the night sky. 'Can you see it? It's moving from left to right. It's just passing the Saucepan.'

'Got it,' he said, breathing in her fragrance. 'I really missed seeing the southern sky when I was in the States.'

She turned her face towards him. 'What did you miss the most?' she asked.

He put an arm around her shoulders and pulled her closer. 'Lots of things,' he said. 'The smell of the dust when the rain first falls in the bush, the sound of kookaburras at dawn and sunset, the sound of rain falling on a tin roof back at home.'

She traced each of his eyebrows with a fingertip. 'Have you ever thought of working in the bush?' she asked.

He captured her finger and pressed a soft kiss to the end of it. 'Yes, of course, but I'm so highly trained now I'm of more use in the city. It's ironic really as the only reason I became a transplant surgeon was to help people like my mother who couldn't access services in time.'

'Why did you become a heart-lung transplant surgeon?' she asked. 'I thought you were planning on specialising in renal surgery?'

'I had a great mentor in the States,' he said. 'He encouraged me to choose the heart-lung route. He thought my skills were more appropriate for heart-lung transplants. It's more challenging surgery. You need nerves of steel. You need to be able to maintain control under impossible circumstances. You have to be able to switch off your feelings and concentrate on the mechanics of the operation. Not everyone can do it.'

'What if there was a fund to help country people?' she asked.

'There isn't one,' Sam said. 'Bush people mortgage their homes and sell off all their assets to access what city folk take for granted. The expenses are crippling. It's not the medical bills so much but the travel and accommodation. Patients can spend months going back and forth over long distances. It's not within most people's budgets to do that.'

'What if I raised some money for a fund for exactly that purpose?' Lexi asked.

Sam brushed her soft mouth with his thumb. 'Haven't you got enough on your plate already with raising funds for the unit?'

'I can do both,' she said. 'I've already been thinking about raising the funds to buy a house for relatives to stay in, similar to what the children's hospital has. Instead of a fast-food chain funding it, we can do it with charitable donations.'

Sam stroked a finger down the curve of her cheek. 'If you weren't working for the hospital as Head of Events, what else would you be doing?' he asked.

She lowered her gaze, her fingers toying with the collar of his open-necked shirt. 'I'm not sure…'

'You must have some idea,' he said. 'What did you want to be when you were a little girl?

A faraway look came into her eyes as she looked past his left shoulder. 'I wanted to be a ballerina,' she said. 'I wanted to dance on the world's stage. I used to practise in front of my mother's cheval mirror. I dreamed of wearing a sparkling tutu. I dreamed of dancing at a Royal performance. I pretended I was Cinderella…' Her voice trailed away and her shoulders dropped.

'So what happened?'

She let out a sigh and went back to playing with the buttons on his shirt. 'My feet got sore.'

Sam lifted her chin. 'If that was the case there would be no ballerinas in the world.'

She looked at him with sad blue eyes. 'I couldn't do that to Bella,' she said. 'She used to look at me so wistfully when I got taken to my ballet class by our nanny. She would sit on the sidelines and watch with those sad grey eyes of hers. She didn't do it intentionally. She's not like that. But I felt so guilty. I had to stop. I had to stop a lot of things I loved… It's kind of been the story of my life.'

Sam had heard similar stories throughout his professional life but none had touched him more than Lexi's. She had given up so much to protect her sister. Did anyone realise how much she had sacrificed?

Her father?

Her mother?

Her older sister Evie?

Even Sam hadn't properly understood until now. There was probably a litany of things she had sacrificed in her effort to protect Bella from feeling inadequate. 'You're a very sweet person, Lexi,' he said. 'But why do you always hide behind that I-don't-give-a-damn-what-you-think facade?'

'Because sometimes it's easier to pretend I don't care,' she said. 'I've got used to putting my feelings to one side.' She gave him a little twisted smile. 'Maybe I'm like you in that regard. I can switch off my feelings when it suits me.'

Sam felt like he had just been hoisted with his own petard. 'It's not always as easy as I make it look,' he said, frowning at her.

'What are you saying, Sam?' she asked with an arch of a slim brow. 'That you sometimes feel more than you let on?'

He held her ocean-blue gaze, determined to outstare her. 'I can't give you what you want,' he said. 'I'm not the right person for you. I've never been the right person.'

She got up and moved a few feet away, finally turning to stand and look at him from the mast, her expression cool and distant. 'Are you the right person for anyone?' she asked.

Sam looked out over the crinkled sea gilded by the silvery moon that had come up. 'When my mother died my father never really got over the loss. I know for a fact he blames himself. They didn't have the money to send her to the city for help. For the last twenty years he's lived like a hermit. I don't think he's ever looked at another woman. Can you imagine that? Twenty years he's lived like a monk because he can't bear the thought of replacing my mother.'

'He must have loved her very much,' Lexi said softly.

Sam let out a hissing breath. 'That's exactly my point,' he said. 'He loved her too much. She wouldn't have wanted him to waste his life like that. She would've wanted him to move on, to find someone else to build a future with, maybe even have another child or two, someone who could take on the farm since I had other plans.'

'Maybe there is no one else who can take your mother's place,' Lexi said. 'Maybe your father has always known that in his heart. Maybe he's perfectly happy living with his memories of their time together.'

Sam frowned at her darkly. 'He should've moved on by now.'

'Why should he?' she asked. 'Is it so hard for you to realise that his love for your mother was enough to satisfy him for a lifetime?'

'I can't imagine loving someone like that,' he said almost savagely. 'It's not what I want for myself.'

'I feel sorry for you, Sam,' Lexi said. 'You've closed yourself off in case you get hurt. But life is all about being hurt. It's not something we can control. There's no switch we can turn off to stop us feeling the pain of losing someone, of loving someone so much we don't feel we can go on without them. We grieve because we love. We might as well be dead if we didn't feel something. It's what makes us all human.'

Sam looked at her standing there, the angles and contours of her beautiful face cast in an ethereal glow by the moonlight. She looked like a mermaid that had come up from the depths of the sea. Her long hair had worked itself loose from the knot she had restrained it in earlier. It was lying about her shoulders and down her back in a silky tangle that his fingers itched to run through. 'Do you love your fiancé like that?' he asked, hating himself for asking it, hating himself even more for wanting to know.

Her eyes moved away from his. She stood stiffly, her gaze on the dark endless sea that moved like a ripple of silk under the caress of the light late-night breeze. 'What I feel for Matthew is nothing to do with you,' she said.

'So you're still going to marry him.'

'Is that a question or a statement?' she asked as she turned and met his gaze, hers diamond-sharp.

'Which would you answer with the truth?' he asked.

She turned away from him to look back to the wrinkled black blanket of the ocean. 'I don't have to tell you anything,' she said. 'I'm just here for now. That's what you want, isn't it? Something casual and temporary. No strings. No feelings. Just a physical connection you could get with anybody.'

'Not just anybody,' he said, coming up behind her to cup her upper arms with his hands. 'It doesn't feel quite like this with anyone else.'

Lexi closed her eyes as she felt his body brush

against hers from behind. His mouth was already at her ear lobe, his teeth tugging at her in playful little bites that sent arrows of delight down her spine. He lifted her hair off the nape of her neck and kissed her there in soft movements of his lips against her super-sensitive skin. She shivered in delight, her whole body alert to the proud jut of his erection pressing against her bottom. She leaned back into him, her head lolling to one side as he worked his magical mouth on her neck.

Did he mean it?

Was *she* the only one who made him feel like this?

Lexi didn't know for sure but when she turned in his embrace and offered her mouth to his, she knew with absolute certainty that she would treasure every moment of this weekend with him, for she suspected these memories would be all she would have of him once it was over.

The rest of the time out on the water with Sam was like a fantasy come to life. Sleeping in Sam's arms at night to the gentle rocking of the yacht was like a dream come true. Waking to his caresses, to the hot urgency of his mouth and hands and surging male body had made her soar to the heights of human pleasure.

Watching the sun come up together made her feel close to Sam in a way she had not felt before. She had never seen him in such a relaxed and playful mood. It was as if he was determined to make this short time together as pleasurable for her as possible. There was no further mention of the past or her engagement. It was a no-go area they had seemed to reach by tacit agreement. Lexi was relieved for she knew she had some hard thinking to do in the days ahead, but for now she was content to treasure every precious second with him.

When the wind came up Sam taught her how to sail, showing her how to go about by ducking under the boom and reeling in the ropes. It was an exhilarating experience and one she knew she would never forget. They had a picnic on an isolated beach that Lexi hadn't even known existed. They swam, but not for long as the water hadn't yet warmed up enough to be comfortable, but Lexi soon grew warm again when Sam enveloped her in his arms and made love to her on the sand.

But eventually the weekend drew to a close. It had to.

Sam's relaxed mood seemed to dissipate the closer they got to the marina on Sunday afternoon. His features took on a cast of stone and when he smiled at something she said it didn't reach his eyes.

Lexi watched as he steered the yacht back into its mooring position. Once it was secured and locked up he helped her step onto the marina walkway and carried her bags of shopping for her. They got to the end of the walkway and an awkward silence fell.

'I'll give you a lift home,' Sam said, not looking at her.

'No… Thanks anyway but I'd better make my own way back,' Lexi said.

Another painful silence passed.

'I guess I'll see you at the hospital,' Sam said, his expression still inscrutable.

'Guess so,' Lexi said, forcing brightness into

her tone. 'And the ball. I can't believe it's next weekend. Have you got a mask to wear?'

'I'm working on it.'

Lexi shifted her weight from foot to foot. 'I had a great time,' she said, looking up at him. 'Thanks for...for everything...'

'Pleasure.'

Well, there had certainly been plenty of that, Lexi thought. Her body was still tingling inside and out.

She started to walk away but Sam suddenly snagged one of her wrists and turned her back to face him. She looked into his unfathomable dark brown eyes and felt her heart trip. 'I want to see you again,' he said, the words low and deep as if they had been sourced from somewhere deep inside him.

Lexi moistened her suddenly dry lips. 'Sam... This is not exactly easy for me...'

A flinty look came into his eyes. 'What's not easy?' he asked. 'Hasn't the last day and a half proved anything to you?'

Lexi drew in an uneven breath, hope flickering inside her chest like a tiny candle flame in a stiff breeze. 'I'm not quite sure what it is you're offering…'

'You know damn well what I'm offering,' he said. 'I'm offering you the most passionate, pleasurable experience of your life.'

'An affair.' It wasn't a question or a statement but an expression of heart-wrenching disappointment. Pain hurtled through her like a cannonball, knocking over all her hopes and dreams like ninepins. He didn't want her for ever. He never had. But in spite of the roaring passion that existed between them it still worried her to think he only wanted her now because someone else had already staked a claim.

'I've always been clear on what I can and can't give you, Lexi,' he said. 'I haven't made any false promises to you and I'm not going to make them to you now.'

'I know,' she said on a sigh that prickled her chest. 'I know…'

He brushed her cheek with the back of his bent knuckles, his eyes gentle and warm as they meshed with hers. 'If ever you need a hideaway

I'll keep that cupboard empty just for you,' he said.

Lexi gave him a bittersweet smile. 'You do that, country boy.' And then she picked up her bags and left to make her way home.

CHAPTER TEN

FINN Kennedy was just about to go home before his throbbing headache turned into a migraine when he got a call from Evie in A and E. He had been having trouble with his arm all day. He had dropped a coffee cup in the doctors' room but thankfully no one had seen it. The pain behind his eyeballs was like dressmaking pins stabbing at him as he tried to concentrate on what Evie was saying.

'We've got a post-op patient of yours in,' she said. 'A Mr Ian Reid with a swelling in his groin. You did a heart-valve op on him eight days ago. He's in pain and the swelling's getting bigger. I think you need to see him.'

Finn rubbed at his aching temple for a moment. The last thing he wanted to do was head into Theatre feeling the way he did just now. What if his arm let him down at a crucial moment? Dropping a coffee cup was one thing, severing an artery was another. 'I'll be down to see him in a few minutes,' he said. 'I have a patient in ICU I have to check on first.'

'We're pretty busy down here,' Evie said. 'The ambos have rung ahead about a stabbing coming in any minute.'

Finn ground his teeth. 'I said I'd be down there, Evie. Just give me five minutes, OK?'

The phone slammed down in his ear.

Finn walked into the cubicle where Ian Reid was propped up in bed, having just finished a sandwich and a cup of tea. A young nurse, Kate Henderson, was just about to clear the tray away.

'Would you like another drink, Mr Reid?' Kate asked.

Finn glared at the nurse as he indicated for her to leave the cubicle to speak to him away from the patient. 'How could you be so stupid as to have fed this patient?' he roared. 'What the hell are you thinking? He's come in with an obvious hematoma over his femoral puncture site, he's obviously still bleeding, he obviously needs emergency surgery, and you're serving him high tea, for God's sake!'

Kate blushed to the roots of her hair and her chin started to wobble uncontrollably. 'But he was hungry, Dr Kennedy. I didn't know he was going to Theatre.'

'Didn't Dr Lockheart inform you of his condition?' Finn asked, frowning furiously.

'Um…she mentioned to make him comfortable until you arrived,' Kate said.

'Comfortable?' Finn said with a sneer. 'Well, he's not going to be very comfortable if he vomits when he's anesthetised, aspirates and ends up on a ventilator in Intensive Care, is he?'

'But I didn't know he needed Theatre…'

'Well, you damn well should have checked,' Finn said. 'Anyone with any sense and experience could tell he was in dire straits and would've taken the initiative to fast him. What are they teaching you lot at university?'

Kate started to cry, her shoulders shaking as she stood with her head bowed before him.

'Oh, for pity's sake,' Finn said. 'Stop acting like a child and get an orderly down here and have them get this patient up to Theatre before any more harm is done. He'll have to have a crash induction and we'll just have to hope to hell nothing goes wrong before we get this bleeding under control.'

Kate scurried off, still brushing at her eyes as she went.

Evie frowned and followed Finn into the office, closing the door for privacy. 'What was that all about?' she asked.

Finn began writing up his patient notes and didn't even acknowledge her with a look. 'What was what all about?' he asked.

Evie ground her teeth as she took in his devil-may-care demeanour. 'You had no right to speak to that young nurse like that,' she said. 'This is only her second day in the department. She's still finding her feet.'

Finn scrawled his signature on the foot of the page before he cut his hard, ice-blue gaze to hers. 'She can find her feet somewhere else,' he said. 'I haven't got time to babysit silly little schoolgirls.'

'That's hardly fair, Finn, you know how hard it is for the new graduates these days,' Evie said. 'They don't have a lot of on-the-ground experience when they come to us.'

Finn gave her a hard look. 'Then you should

be watching for slip-ups like this. It's my name that will be dragged through the courts on a malpractice suit if something goes wrong. What the hell are you doing down here? Running a bloody crèche?'

Evie flattened her mouth in annoyance. 'You really get off on intimidating everyone, don't you?' she asked.

He eyeballed her for so long the air almost started to pulse with tension. 'You want to pick a fight, princess?' he asked. 'Just keep going the way you are.'

She stood her ground, even though her stomach gave a funny little wobble as his ice-pick gaze pinned hers. 'Why do you do it, Finn? Why are you so determined to alienate everyone?'

His eyes were like stone as they held hers, his jaw just as unmalleable. 'I'm not here to win a popularity contest.'

'Maybe not,' she said. 'But it doesn't mean you can't demonstrate a bit of emotional intelligence from time to time, especially with younger members of staff. You're meant to be a role model. Monkey see, monkey do, remember?'

'Leave it, Evie,' he said, tossing the file on

the desk with an impatient flick of his hand, his forehead crisscrossed with a brooding frown.

'No, I will not leave it, Finn,' she said. 'You can't come into my department and throw your weight around, or at least not on my watch.'

His lip curled upwards in a smirk as he stepped towards her. 'Your watch?' he asked. 'Since when have you been appointed Department Head?'

Evie was the only thing between him and the door and she was determined not to move until she had said her piece. But it was hard work staring him down when he was so big and so threatening and so very close. She could feel the heat coming off his body. She could smell his scent: one part aftershave and three parts potent, hard-working male. She could feel herself responding to his nearness. She could feel her skin prickling as he sent his gaze on an indolent perusal of her body. Those Antarctic, unreachable, unreadable eyes seemed to be slowly but surely stripping her of every stitch of clothing, leaving spot fires burning in their wake. 'I might not be a head of department but I'm responsible for the staff who work with me,' she said, trying to keep her voice steady. 'It's about being a team. We're meant to be working together, not against one another.'

Finn's hooded gaze burned into hers. 'You want to get out of my way, princess?'

Evie felt a warning shiver scurry down her spine like a small furry animal but she still didn't budge. A perverse desire to get under his skin kept egging her on. 'What are you going to do, Finn?' she asked. 'Throw me over your shoulder, caveman style?'

His eyes gleamed menacingly and she felt his warm breath skate over her uptilted face. 'Now, that sounds like a plan,' he said, planting a hand either side of her head, trapping her within the cage of his strong arms.

Evie sucked in a quick little breath that felt like it had tiny rose thorns attached as he moved just that little bit closer. His hard, muscular chest brushed against the swell of her breasts and his belt buckle poked her in the belly, an erotic hint of what would happen if she allowed him any nearer. Her body flared with heat at his disturbing proximity, her skin tingling with awareness, her scalp prickling all over. His eyes were a deep and dangerous blue sea of male desire as they held hers. Her heart started to flap at the wall of her chest like a shredded truck tyre against bitumen. And her mouth went totally dry as his loomed inexorably closer…

A rumble of voices in the background suddenly lifted Finn's head. 'Might want to open that door, Evie,' he drawled mockingly as he stepped back from her. 'Your *team* might be wondering what's keeping you from doing your job.'

Evie moved aside to let him pass, her heart still flip-flopping against her ribcage as she sent him a contentious glare. 'Go to hell, Finn.'

He flicked her cheek with a lazy finger on the way past. 'Been there, done that and thrown away the T-shirt long, long ago,' he said, and then he left.

'What's been eating at Finn Kennedy lately?' Julie, one of the nurses on duty, asked Evie a little while later as they were clearing up a cubicle after a patient had been transferred to ICU. 'He's been wandering around like a bear with a sore head.'

Evie peeled off her gloves and tossed them in

the bin. 'I have no idea,' she said. 'He's always been a law unto himself.'

A head popped through the curtains from the next cubicle. It was one of the other nurses who had worked with Finn earlier. 'That's because he *has* got a sore head,' she said. 'I saw him pop a couple of paracetamol before he left. Mind you, who wouldn't get a headache working here? Patients are lined up three deep in the waiting room and there are no beds.'

Evie frowned. 'Finn had a headache?'

The nurse nodded. 'He saw me looking at him while he was getting the painkillers and said he was fighting a migraine.'

Evie let out a breath and sank her teeth into her bottom lip. 'He should have said something…'

Julie gave a snort as she bundled up the linen in her arms. 'Yeah, right, that sounds like something Finn Kennedy would do.'

Evie took off her stethoscope and ran the rubber tubing through her fingers. Finn had seemed particularly snarly this evening. And she had gone at him all guns blazing. If he was struggling with a migraine it was no wonder he had lost his temper with the junior nurse. And he'd had to take Mr Reid to Theatre. It would have been a nightmare for him if he hadn't been feeling well.

She glanced at her watch. Her shift was nearly over. It was late but not too late to deliver an apology in person.

Finn's penthouse apartment light was on. Evie had checked before she had knocked on the door but it seemed a decade or two before he answered.

The door swung open and he scowled down at her. 'What do you want?'

'How's your headache?' she asked.

His frown deepened. 'What headache?'

'The headache that made you act like an absolute boor in A and E earlier this evening,' she said.

His hand fell away from the door and tunnelled through his hair. 'It's fine,' he said in a gruff tone. 'I've taken something for it. It's almost gone.'

Evie sidled past him in the doorway.

'What are you doing?' he asked, shooting her a glare.

'I've come to apologise.'

'For what?'

'For laying into you the way I did,' she said. 'I didn't realise you were ill.'

His brows snapped together. 'I'm not ill.'

'You have a headache.'

'So?'

'Doesn't that qualify as being ill?'

'Not if it doesn't interfere with my work,' he said.

'But it does interfere with your work,' she argued. 'The way you spoke to that poor girl was—'

He opened the door and jerked his head for her to leave. 'Don't let me keep you.'

Evie ignored the open door. 'Have you had migraines before?' she asked.

'Go home, Evie,' he said grimly. 'I don't need a diagnosis. I had a tension headache. I get them occasionally. Everyone does. Now leave.'

'There have been a number of times at work when I've seen you struggling with your coordination,' she said. 'I've seen you drop things. And that facial stitching you abandoned that time? It was like you couldn't get your fingers to work. Now you're having migraines. Have you thought of having some scans done to rule out anything sinister?'

Finn let out an impatient curse. 'I haven't got a brain tumour,' he said. 'I haven't got anything. Now get out of here before I lose my temper.'

Evie moved even further into his apartment, trailing her fingers over the leather sofa as she walked by to look out of the bank of windows overlooking the harbour. She affected an air of calm she was nowhere near feeling. Finn was intimidating at the best of times, but in this mood he was lethal. He reminded her of an alpha wolf who had taken himself away to lick his wounds without the cynosure of critical eyes. The thing she had to establish was if the wound he was hiding was self-inflicted. That was the one question she dreaded asking but ask it she must.

'What the hell do you think you're doing?' Finn asked.

Evie turned and looked at him, taking a deep breath before she asked, 'Is it alcohol? Have you got a hangover?'

His expression became thunderous. 'What are you implying?' he asked.

Evie rolled her lips together for a moment. 'You know what people are like, Finn,' she said. 'They talk, gossip, spread rumours.'

'Then they can bloody well talk,' he said. 'I don't drink on the job. Never have, never will.'

'I want to believe you but—'

'I don't give a rat's backside if you believe me or not,' he shot back. 'Now, I'm going to say this one more time. Leave.'

Evie folded her arms and eyeballed him. 'Aren't you going to offer me a cup of coffee or something?'

His face was a blank canvas. 'No.'

'You don't give a damn about anyone, do you?' she asked.

'Not particularly.'

'I'm trying to understand you,' she said, her voice rising in frustration. 'But you're so damned obstructive. Why can't you at least meet me half-way?'

Finn shut the door with a definitive click; the gunshot sound of it making Evie flinch. She drew in an uneven breath as he sauntered over to where she was standing, his long legs eating up the distance in a matter of strides.

His features were harsh as he looked down at her, his cold, unfathomable eyes nailing hers. 'What is it you really want, Evie?' he asked. 'A cosy chat over coffee or a quick tumble in the sack to let off some steam?'

Evie felt her face flash with heat. 'You think I came here to sleep with you?' she asked.

'Yeah, that's what I think.' His eyes flicked to her mouth before coming back to mesh with hers, challenging her, provoking her, *arousing* her.

She straightened her spine and sent him a withering look. 'Strange as it may seem, Finn, I don't want to dive headfirst into your bed,' she said. 'Call me picky but I don't care for where you've been just lately.'

He gave her a devilish smile as he stepped into her body space. She tried to move away but the sofa was in the way. He captured some strands of her hair and looped them around his fingertip, a disturbingly intimate tether that sent her heart into an erratic rhythm. 'Liar,' he said. 'We both know why you're here, princess. You want me to finish what I started back in the office.'

Evie ran her tongue out over the chalk-dry surface of her lips. 'Y-you're totally wrong,' she said in a husky whisper that didn't really help her denial one little bit. 'I just wanted to check that you were all right. I was concerned about you.'

He fisted some of her hair in his hands; the tugging should have been painful but instead it was intensely erotic against her scalp. His eyes dipped to her mouth, lingering there for a heart-stopping moment before he came back to her gaze. 'Keep your concern for someone who wants it,' he said. 'I have no need or desire to be taken care of and certainly not by you.'

'Why must you block anyone getting close to you?' Evie asked.

His fist tightened on her hair, making her toes curl inside her shoes. His eyes blazed with heat as they bored into hers. 'I'm not blocking you now, princess,' he drawled. 'You can get as close to me as you want. I won't stop you.'

Evie snatched in a prickly breath. 'I'm not talking about physical closeness.'

He bent his head to her neck, his lips nibbling on her skin in a teasing caress that sent a shiver down the length of her spine. 'It's the only type of closeness I want,' he said. 'And you want it too, don't you, Evie, hmm?'

Evie wished she could deny it but her legs were already folding beneath her as his tongue moved across her lower jaw, making every nerve spring to attention. She tilted her head to one side to give him better access, her eyes closing as ripples of pleasure flowed through her body. He got closer and closer to her mouth without actually touching her lips. It was a torturous assault on her senses. She felt her lips buzzing with need as he advanced and retreated, again and again and again, until with a little whimper of desperation she finally took matters into her own hands and pressed her mouth to his.

Fireworks went off in her body as he took control of the kiss. His lips moved against hers with bruising pressure, his tongue not asking for entry but taking it in one savage thrust that lifted every hair on her head, including the ones he still had fisted in his hand.

He turned her in one deft movement and began walking her backwards to the nearest wall, his muscled thighs moving against hers in a commanding and totally provocative manner. She felt the surge of his erection against her belly as her back hit the wall, the rock-hard length of him pulsing with the drumbeats of raw, primal, male need. Her body was aflame, her feminine core already seeping with the dew of her longing. It was a raging fever in her blood, a full-throttle rush of sexual need on a scale she had never felt before. She felt wanton and wild with his mouth crushing hers. She gave another whimper as his mouth ground against hers with savage intent, his tongue demanding hers submit to his. She fought him every step of the way for supremacy. She used her teeth, small nippy bites and harder ones, but he refused to allow her control.

'Damn you,' he growled against her mouth as he tugged at her top to uncover her breasts. 'Damn you to hell.'

'Damn you right back,' she said as she held her arms up over her head so he could remove her top with a reckless abandon she suspected she might regret later when common sense returned.

He kicked the top away with his foot as his mouth ground against hers, his hands roughly caressing her breasts through the lace of her bra. It was exhilarating to feel his warm hands on her but she wanted more. She wanted to feel him skin on skin. She wanted no barriers between them.

Evie put her hands behind her back to unhook her bra, letting it drop to the floor at her feet. Finn murmured with approval and left her mouth to suck savagely on her right breast. She gasped out loud at the impact of his hot mouth on her puckered flesh. He swirled his tongue round her nipple, his teeth nipping at her, tugging, pulling and teasing in a cycle of pleasure and pain that had her totally at his mercy. His mouth was ruthless, hot and insistent, determined and dangerous as it toyed with her sensitive flesh.

She didn't waste time on his shirt; instead her hands went straight to the waistband of his trousers, fumbling over the fastening in her desperate haste to feel him under her fingertips. He was so hard it made her insides quiver in a combination of anticipation and trepidation. She could feel the pulsing heart of him pressing against the restraint of the fabric of his underwear as she undid his zipper.

A hot burst enflamed her insides as she finally uncovered him. The arrantly male jut of his body was smooth as satin but as hard as steel. Her hand moved up and down his length, slowly at first, exploring him, delighting in how aroused he was.

He gave a guttural groan and wrenched her hand away, pushing her almost roughly back against the wall as he lifted her skirt, his fingers pushing aside her knickers to slip with devastating thoroughness into the hot, wet heart of her.

Evie arched up in aching need to feel more, to have more of him, to have all of him. She could feel the tension building inside her, the dizzying rush of her blood, the emptying of her brain but for the fiery sensations coursing through her.

His mouth came back to hers in a hard kiss that had an undertow of desperation in it. His tongue duelled with hers in an erotic mimic of how he wanted to possess her. Her body thrilled at the sensual promise, the inner walls of her core pulsing with the need to feel him moving inside her. Every nerve in her body was screaming for more. For more of his touch, for more of his branding kisses, for the release she wanted more than her next breath.

He made another rough male sound deep in

his throat as she moved urgently against him. He hoisted one of her legs around his waist, positioning himself before driving so deeply into her silky warmth her head banged against the wall.

Her gasp was swallowed by his mouth as it plundered hers. The friction of his body within hers sent shockwaves of delight through her. She felt pleasure in every part of her from her curling toes to her prickling scalp where one of his hands had locked onto her hair to anchor himself.

It was a rough coupling, a desperate, urgent mating that bordered on animalistic. He thrust deeper and deeper, and harder and harder, his breath a hot gust near her ear as he laboured over her.

Evie felt the first faint flutters of orgasm, the tiny ripples that rolled through her, gathering speed with each pounding movement of his body within hers. She felt her body chase the delicious feeling, all her intimate muscles tensing for the freefall into ecstasy.

Suddenly it consumed her.

It picked her up like a giant wave and thrashed

her about before spitting her out the other side, spent and limbless.

She was so sensitised she felt every pulsing moment of Finn's release. She felt the way his body tensed all over before that final explosive plunge into his own paradise. Her inner core felt each and every aftershock and her mouth accepted each and every earthy gasp from his.

Evie felt him slump against her, his head buried against her neck, his breathing ragged and un-even. Her hands slipped under the loose tails of his shirt, her fingertips memorising every knob of his vertebrae. He flinched as she touched him between his shoulder blades so she backed off. But then she felt the puckered flesh of the scar he had sustained during combat and her fingers stalled…

As if he sensed her hesitation he pulled back from her, his expression shuttered as he refastened his trousers. 'You should have gone home when I told you to,' he said.

'I don't like being told what to do,' she said. 'You should know that by now.'

'Here,' he said, tossing her bra and top at her. 'Get dressed.'

Her heart sank. But what had she expected? Evie considered defying him but decided against it. Somehow having a discussion with her topless and him fully clothed didn't really appeal. Once she was decent she turned and searched his features. Was he really so cold he could push her out the door as if nothing had happened between them just now? It might have been rough sex. It might have been rushed and raw and performed with most of their clothes still on, but it had been the best sex she'd ever had. For a brief moment she had felt a connection with him that had superseded the mere physical. She had felt his vulnerability in their passionate embrace, the way he had lost himself in her body as if she was the only one who could reach inside him and soothe and comfort the dark bleakness of his soul.

'Let me see it,' she said softly. 'Let me see your scar.'

He scowled at her menacingly. 'I'm not a freak show, Evie. You got what you came for, now get the hell out of here.'

Evie dug her heels in. Any reaction from him

was better than no reaction. Red-hot anger was better than chilly indifference. 'You got that when your brother was killed, didn't you?' she asked. 'You were almost killed as well.'

His jaw clicked as he ground his teeth. 'Get out.'

'You feel guilty that he died instead of you,' she went on. 'That's why you punish yourself by working such crazy hours. You close yourself off from everyone because you don't believe you deserve to be happy because you lived and he didn't.'

She saw his hands clench into fists and a vein bulge in his neck. His eyes were blue chips of ice, hard and unyielding, distant, closed off, angry. 'Get out before I throw you out,' he ground out.

Evie raised her chin. 'I think you care about people way more than you let on,' she said. 'Take me, for instance.'

His lip curled mockingly. 'I just did.'

A dagger pierced her heart but she went on regardless. 'You hate yourself for needing anyone. You keep everything and everyone on a clinical basis. We just had amazing sex and yet you just trivialised it as if it meant nothing. You cheapened it as if I was just another girl you picked up at a bar. But I'm not just another one-night stand. I'm someone who cares about you. Don't ask me why but I do.'

He gave her a flinty look. 'Are you done?'

Evie let out a breath. 'You don't believe me, do you? You don't believe anyone can care about you. Why do you believe that? Why do you think you're so unworthy of love?'

'Love?' He spat the word out as if it was acid. 'Is that how you have to justify what we just did? You're using the wrong four-letter word, princess. What we just did was have a good old fashioned—'

Evie closed her eyes as if that would stop her hearing the coarse word, but of course it didn't. She opened them again to see him looking at her with that same mocking expression. She felt hurt beyond description. She was nothing to him other than a sexual outlet, one of many he had used. Their intimacy hadn't touched him at all. She had imagined it. Her overwhelming attraction to him had distorted her judgement. She felt used, cheap, like a piece of trash he no longer had any use for. 'You really are a piece of work, aren't you, Finn?' she said with an embittered look.

He leaned indolently against the sofa, his eyes running over her lasciviously, smoulderingly. 'You ever feel that itch again, princess, just knock on my door and I'll gladly be of service,' he said.

She turned for the door, wrenching it open before she threw him a glittering look over her shoulder. 'Don't hold your breath,' she said, slamming the door behind her.

Finn pushed himself away from the sofa, cursing. He had just broken his own code with Evie. Evie, of all people! He should have known she wasn't the type of woman to play by his rules. It would never be just sex with Evie Lockheart. She pushed against his boundaries in a hundred different ways with her concerned looks and soft voice and those velvet hands touching him as if he was the most fascinating specimen of manhood. For a moment there he had lost himself in her.

Totally lost himself.

Felt things that he had no right to be feeling.

He didn't do feelings.

He didn't do emotional connection.

He didn't want to feel anything for her. And he certainly didn't want her feeling anything for him. But the sex had been mind-blowing, even if it had lacked finesse. All he had wanted to do was bury himself in her and forget about everything except the way his body felt gripped tightly by hers.

And it had felt incredible.

She had met him physically in a way he had not expected. Her body had been so responsive to his. He had felt every silky ripple of her skin, every tight spasm of her orgasm, every breathless gasp of her breath into his mouth as he'd driven them both into oblivion.

It had been much more than a meeting of bodies in the primal act of mating. He had felt the stirrings of a much deeper bonding that had terrified him. Evie had revealed her vulnerable side, citing feelings for him he had never asked for, never sought, and secretly dreaded.

He had a feeling she could see inside him, the *real* inside—the inside where the ragged edges of his soul barely held him together any more. His emotional centre had been bludgeoned in childhood and then obliterated completely the day Isaac had died.

He was dead inside, dead emotionally. But Evie with her soft hazel eyes kept stroking at the cold heart of him with her looks of concern and her questions about his health. It was as if she was determined to perform cardiac massage on his lifeless soul.

Allowing someone, *anyone*, into the locked and bolted heart of him was unthinkable. He never wanted to feel anything for anyone again. He didn't want anyone to feel anything for him either because he was sure he would only let them down just as he had his brother.

He was used to being alone.

It was the only place where he truly felt safe.

CHAPTER ELEVEN

'YOU won't believe the juicy piece of gossip I heard on the weekend,' Lexi's assistant Jane said as soon as Lexi came in on Monday morning.

Lexi kept her expression blank but her heart gave a little stumble of panic. 'Oh?' she said offhandedly as she leafed through some donation slips.

'Your sister and Finn Kennedy had a blazing row in A and E,' Jane said. 'They tore strips off each other.'

'So?' Lexi said, privately releasing a sigh of relief the gossip hadn't been about her and Sam. 'It's not the first time they've locked heads and it probably won't be the last.'

'Yes, but that's not all,' Jane said. 'Finn had her backed up against the door in the office and it looked like he was about to kiss her. It was only because one of the staff came past that he didn't.'

'I still don't think that means they're an item,' Lexi said.

Jane leaned forward conspiratorially. 'Not only that. Evie went to his apartment later that night. One of the nurses who lives in the same block saw her.'

Lexi put the donation slips down and gave Jane a look of reproach. 'That doesn't mean anything. She might've gone there to talk about a patient or something, or maybe she went there to try and smooth things over.'

'Can't have worked 'cause they're still at loggerheads,' Jane said. 'Everyone's talking about it. Mind you, I can see what she sees in him. He's seriously gorgeous with that sexy stubble and that haven't-slept-properly-in-weeks look. What woman wouldn't want to jump into bed with him?'

Lexi had her own complicated love life to deal with without getting embroiled in her sister's, but when she happened to run into Evie in one of the staffroom bathrooms a couple of days later it was obvious Evie had something on her mind.

'Lexi, I want a word with you,' Evie said,

blocking the main door with her body so no one could disturb them.

'Sure,' Lexi said. 'What's up?'

Evie narrowed her eyes at her. 'What the hell are you up to with Sam Bailey?'

Lexi felt her chest freeze in mid-inhalation. 'I'm not sure what you mean.'

'You don't?' Evie said with a raised brow. 'Well, how about I spell it out for you? I was on late shift last night with an intern who happened to be working on his father's boat at the weekend. He said he saw you getting on Sam's boat on Saturday afternoon. He also said he saw you leaving it the following evening.'

Lexi chewed at the inside of her bottom lip. 'I know it looks bad...'

'Bad?' Evie's tone was incredulous. 'Do you realise what'll happen if this does the rounds of the hospital? You're putting everything in jeopardy. Your engagement, your work for the transplant unit, not to mention Sam's reputation. Do you realise that?'

'What about you?' Lexi said, going on the defensive. 'Everyone is talking about you going to Finn's apartment late at night. Do you want to tell me what time you left or is that no one's business but your own?'

Evie's mouth flattened. 'At least I'm not supposed to be marrying another man next month. You can't have it both ways, Lexi. You have to make up your mind. Matthew doesn't deserve this.'

'I know, I know, but I'm so confused,' Lexi said, fighting tears. 'I can't get a call through to him to even talk to him. What am I supposed to do? Send him an email or a text and tell him I'm in love with someone else?'

Evie's shoulders dropped as she let out a sigh. 'God, I didn't realise things were that bad,' she said. 'You really love him…Sam, I mean?'

Lexi nodded miserably.

'And what does Sam feel?' Evie asked. 'Does he love you?'

'No…' Lexi's chin wobbled. 'He's never loved me.'

Evie let out another sigh and reached for Lexi, hugging her tightly. 'Then you've got yourself one hell of a problem, hon,' she said.

'Tell me about it,' Lexi said, and burst into tears.

* * *

The night of the ball finally arrived. The marquee at the front of the hospital looked spectacular. Starched white linen tablecloths adorned each table set with gleaming silverware and crystal glasses. Black and gold satin ribbons festooned the chairs and crystal candelabra centrepieces gave each table an old-world charm.

The press had arrived to document the event, cameras flashing everywhere just like at a Hollywood premier as the guests walked up the red carpet accompanied by the beautiful music of a string quartet.

The men were dressed in black tie suits, the women in gorgeous evening gowns, and almost everyone had entered into the spirit of the occasion by donning a mask.

Lexi was wearing a backless silver satin gown, nipped in at the waist and floating to the floor in a small but elegant train. She had chosen a Venetian mask, which covered most of her face, and her hair she'd had professionally styled in a glamorous pile on top of her head.

Evie had arrived and had spoken briefly to Lexi but she seemed to be doing her best to avoid

Finn, who looked particularly dashing in a mask that only revealed his piercing ice-blue eyes.

Lexi knew the exact moment when Sam arrived. The fine hairs on the back of her neck lifted and she swung her eyes to the entrance of the marquee where she found him looking straight at her. The slow burn of his gaze made her feel as if he was seeing right through her evening gown to the tiny strip of lace that was her only item of underwear.

He looked magnificent in a black tuxedo, and the black highwayman's mask he was wearing gave him a devilishly sexy look that made a hot flood of desire rush over the floor of her stomach and flow tantalisingly between her thighs.

He looked away to respond to another guest who had spoken to him, and Lexi took a much-needed sip of her champagne to settle her nerves.

Other guests came in and drinks and canapés were served. Some masks had to be removed for guests to eat and drink, but they were still a great ice-breaker and everyone seemed to be having fun as they perused the silent-auction items set up along one wall of the marquee.

The evening progressed with a fork-food buffet

dinner, which Lexi had specifically organised so people could mingle rather than be stuck at one table. The dancing had already started and the music was upbeat and got even the most determined wallflowers up on their feet. Lexi could see Sam dancing with Suzy Carpenter, one of the nurses with a reputation for sleeping around. Lexi wondered if Sam would be one of Suzy's conquests by the time the night was over. It certainly looked like that was Suzy's goal if the way she was draping herself all over him was any indication, Lexi thought, turning away in disgust.

Lexi had so far been too busy seeing that everything ran smoothly to get on the dance floor herself, but then she heard the band strike up the opening bars of the song that had been her first dance with Sam on the night they had met five years ago. A rush of emotion filled her, and she quickly walked out of the marquee, not sure she could bear seeing Sam dance their song with someone else.

She was standing looking at the view of the harbour when she felt someone come up behind her. 'They're playing our song,' Sam said, his broad shoulder brushing hers.

Lexi turned and looked up at him. 'You remembered?'

He held out his arms for her to step into them with a crooked smile on his face. 'How could I forget?'

She stepped into his arms and sighed as her body came up against his. She laid her head on his chest and moved with him as the slow romantic ballad took her back in time. 'I've missed you,' Lexi said. 'I can't stop thinking about the weekend, how wonderful it was.'

Sam rested his chin on the top of her head as the song changed to a poignant minor key. 'I've missed you too,' he said, his legs moving in time with hers.

They danced through another number, a slow waltz that made Lexi feel like she was floating on air instead of dancing with her feet firmly on the ground. It always felt like that in Sam's arms. Her worries and cares slipped to the back of her mind when his arms held her close against him. She felt protected and safe, his arms like a shield to keep the world and all its disappointments away from her. He might not love her the way she wanted to be loved but she was sure he felt something for her, something more than just transient lust. But would it be enough to sustain a relationship between them? And for how long? A week or two? A month? Three months?

And what was she going to do about Matthew? He had promised to match the funds she raised this evening. How could she tell him she no longer wanted to marry him? How could she reach him before she went any further with Sam?

Lexi felt Sam's lips moving against her hair. 'What are you doing after this is over?' he asked. 'Do you want to come and spend the night with me on my yacht? Tomorrow we could go out on the water. Just the two of us. No interruptions.'

Lexi looked up into his handsome face. 'Sam…'

A frown settled between his brows. 'You haven't told your fiancé yet, have you?'

She lowered her gaze, staring at the bow tie at his neck rather than meet his gaze. 'I have responsibilities, Sam. I've made a commitment to the hospital and I can't just walk away. It's not that simple. People are relying on me.'

Sam's features darkened with cynicism. 'It's about the money, isn't it?' he said. 'You'd do anything for Brentwood's money, wouldn't you? You'd even sell your soul.'

Lexi stepped back and hugged her upper arms against the light chill in the air. 'Sam, you're asking too much and giving too little,' she said. 'You want me to give up my life for you but what are you promising in return?'

His eyes glittered darkly. 'Isn't what we have together enough for now?' he asked.

Lexi opened her mouth to answer when she heard the sound of footsteps and two male voices approaching.

One was her father's.

'I think she went out there,' Richard said. 'She's probably gone off to the kitchen to sort something out with the caterers. She won't be far away. Do you want me to call her on her mobile? I'm pretty sure she has it switched on.'

The other voice was her fiancé's.

'No,' Matthew Brentwood said, anticipation and excitement evident in his voice. 'Don't do that. She has no idea I'm here. She walked past me three times already and didn't recognise me. I want it to be a surprise when I finally take off my mask.'

Lexi looked at Sam in wide-eyed panic. *Matthew was here?* Her heart threatened to beat its way out of her chest. She couldn't breathe. She felt trapped. Claustrophobic. Her stomach was churning. She wasn't prepared. She needed more time. She needed to get her emotions in check.

Sam gave her a look that cut her to ribbons. 'Thank you for the dance,' he said. 'I hope you enjoy the rest of your evening.' And without another word he strode away, not back into the marquee where all the laughter and music and frivolity was happening but into the anonymous darkness of the night.

CHAPTER TWELVE

IT TOOK Lexi over a week to find the courage to tell Matthew their engagement was over. It was the worst feeling in the world to have broken someone's heart, and not just Matthew's heart but his parents' and sisters' too.

After she had said spoken to Matthew she stood outside the Brentwoods' lovely family home, the house she had come to think of as her second home, and knew she would never be back.

It would have been easier if Matthew had been angry at her, furious with her for betraying him. But instead he had just been sad, utterly and indescribably sad. His grey-blue eyes had looked stricken as she had told him she couldn't marry him. He hadn't shouted. He hadn't hurled abuse at her. He hadn't even withdrawn his offer of matching the amount of money she had raised for the transplant unit. He had honoured his promise, which made the breaking of hers that much harder for her to do without feeling appallingly guilty, even though she knew deep in her heart she was doing the right thing.

As soon as Lexi's father found out he told her to pack her bags and leave. He ranted and raved, shouting and swearing, thumping his fists on the table, reminding Lexi of a child having a tantrum because he couldn't have his own way. Unable to bear it any longer, she packed a few things before she made her way to Sam's apartment.

She rang the doorbell but there was no answer. A sickening feeling of déjà vu assailed her. Surely he hadn't left without telling her? But of course not, she reassured herself. He was working at the hospital. He had a two-year contract with an option for five. He was probably on call or something.

Sam wasn't at the hospital either, Susanne, his practice manager, informed her. 'He had a heart-lung transplant this morning,' she said. 'He did his rounds straight after he saw a few patients in the rooms. You might find him down at the marina. He's probably gone out for a quick sail. He should be just about back by now.'

'Thanks, Susanne.' Lexi turned to leave.

'Oh, and, Lexi?' Susanne said.

Lexi turned at the door. 'Yes?'

'I'm sorry to hear about your engagement,' Susanne said. 'I heard about it from one of the staff.'

'Thank you,' Lexi said. 'But I think it's for the best.'

It was almost sundown by the time Lexi got to the marina. Her heart sank when she couldn't see Sam's boat anywhere in sight. Then in the distance she could see his yacht motoring back to the marina. She drank in the sight of him. She hadn't seen him since the night of the ball. He looked so gorgeous standing at the helm of his boat, steering it into its mooring place.

She stood with her bags at her feet, waiting for him, her heart beating hard and fast in excitement and longing.

He looked up and saw her, a frown carving

into his forehead when his gaze went to the bags at her feet. Once the boat was tied up securely he jumped down on the marina to face her. 'What are you doing here, Lexi?' he asked, still frowning formidably.

Lexi's stomach did a queasy little turnover. 'I've come to tell you I've called off my engagement,' she said.

'I already heard about that in the doctors' room this morning,' he said, as if it was the most insignificant news, like the current price of milk or bread.

Lexi licked her dry lips. 'I would've liked you to have been the first to know but my father took it upon himself to tell everyone what a disappointment for a daughter I've become because I cancelled my wedding within a couple of weeks of the ceremony.'

'It's your life, not his,' he said, his face set like marble.

Lexi let out a rattling breath. 'Sam? Is everything all right?'

His eyes were blank. 'Sure? Why wouldn't it be?'

She bit her lip. 'I just thought you'd be more…

more excited about me ending things with Matthew. I thought you'd be thrilled we can be together now. I'm free, Sam. It can be just you and me. We can be together all the time.'

Sam glanced at her bags before returning his gaze to hers. 'I offered you an affair, not a place to stay,' he said. 'Nothing serious and nothing long term, remember?'

Lexi looked at his mouth speaking those cruel, heartbreaking words and wondered if she had misheard him. She moistened her lips again. 'Sam, I love you. Surely you know that by now? I love you and I want to be with you.'

His jaw was tight, his eyes hard and impenetrable. 'I don't love you, Lexi. I've never loved you. I'm happy to enjoy an affair with you but that's it. Take or leave it.'

Inside Lexi's chest she felt her heart had broken off in a thousand sharp-edged pieces, each one scoring at her lungs every time she took a breath. 'You can't mean that, Sam,' she said, tears building up in her eyes. 'I've given up everything for you. I can't imagine life without you. How can you do this to me?'

Sam's expression was still locked down. 'I

haven't done anything to you, Lexi. You've done it to yourself.'

'You asked me to end my engagement!' She didn't care that her voice was shrill.

'I didn't ask you to do any such thing,' he said in a steely voice. 'I just asked you how you could possibly think of marrying a man who didn't satisfy you. You were marrying him for all the wrong reasons. I did not at any point offer to take his place at the altar.'

Lexi swallowed her anguish with an effort. Pride was the only thing she had left and she clung to it with the desperation a drowning person did a life raft. She would have to walk away. She would have to rebuild her life. She would have to learn to be happy without Sam, the only man she had ever loved, the only man she *could* ever love. There would be no happy ending. No marriage and making babies together. It had all been a fantasy that she had mistaken for the real thing. *Again.* Yet again she had been duped by her own foolish, romantic dreams. 'I hope you find what you're looking for, Sam,' she said in a cold, hard voice. 'And then when you find it,

I hope it gets snatched away from you and you never get it back.' And then she picked up her bags and walked back up the marina, out of his life for good.

Sam watched her walk away, the words to call her back lodged in the middle of his throat where a choking knot had formed. Seeing Lexi on the wharf with her bags packed, ready to move into his life, had made him panic. But, then, ever since he had heard she had called off her engagement he had felt conflicted. He had felt the same gut-wrenching agitation the night of the ball when he'd heard the sound of her fiancé's voice.

Up until that point Sam had assumed Matthew Brentwood was one of those rich, shallow guys who had plucked the prettiest girl from his social set and got engaged to her because it was the thing to do. But hearing Matthew's excitement at seeing Lexi again had hit Sam in the gut like a wildly flung bowling ball.

The man loved her, *really* loved her.

Sam needed time to think, to process what it

meant now Lexi was free. He felt uncomfortable with the prospect of being forever labelled as the man who had come between her and her fiancé, especially when he wasn't sure he could offer her more than a resumption of their affair. He *wanted* to offer more but he didn't know if he was capable of opening up that part of him that had closed down so long ago.

Lexi deserved better than another casual fling with him. She deserved to be loved totally and completely, but he wasn't sure he was ready to make that sort of emotional commitment, or at least not yet.

Sam threw himself into work over the next couple of weeks but even after the most gruelling days he still hadn't been able to sleep at night. He thought about Lexi all the time. He hadn't seen her at the hospital. He had heard via one of the nurses that she had taken some leave. The days seemed so long and pointless without the anticipation of running into her in one of the corridors or on the ward. He hadn't realised how much he had looked forward to those offchance meetings, those little verbal stoushes that had made his blood bubble with sexual excitement in his veins.

Even being out on his boat wasn't the same any more. He could still smell the fragrance of her perfume. It had seemed to permeate the very woodwork of its every surface, torturing him with a thousand little reminders of her: the way she had squealed as she had jumped into the cold water of the ocean; the way her naked body had been wrapped around his on the hot sand as he'd possessed her; the way her soft mouth had pleasured him; the way she had stroked and caressed every inch of his body until he had thought of nothing but the incredible release he felt with her. Even his shirts smelled like her. Wearing them was like wrapping himself in her.

He wanted to rewind the clock, to go back to the marina and do it all differently. But every time he called her phone it went straight to the answering service. And each time he hadn't said anything. Not a word. Hell, it was so pathetic. He had been as tongue-tied as any shy young teenager asking a girl on a first date.

Sam drove up to visit his father on the weekend to distract himself from the habit he'd developed lately of incessantly checking his phone for texts or missed calls. He was acting like some of the teenagers he saw around town, their phones never out of their hands, their fingers constantly texting or scrolling.

Jack Bailey enveloped him in a bear hug as soon as he arrived. 'I hope you don't mind, Sam, but I've invited a young lady to join us for dinner,' he said.

'Come on, Dad,' Sam said with an edge of irritation. 'You know I hate it when you try and hook me up with women. I can find my own dates.' *And lose them, not once but twice.* Would Lexi ever forgive him for that? he wondered. Probably not. No wonder she wasn't taking his calls.

'This one's not for you, son,' Jack said grinning. 'Jean's my date.'

Sam stared at his father with his mouth open. 'You've got a *date*?'

Jack beamed. 'It's only taken me twenty years to put myself out there but she's great, Sam. She reminds me of your mother. I guess that's why I fell in love with her.'

Sam was still gobsmacked. 'You're in love?'

'Yep, and I'm getting married,' Jack said.

'Married?'

Jack nodded happily but then his expression turned sombre. 'I grieved too long for your mum,' he said. 'I guess I felt so guilty about her dying because I couldn't afford the health cover. But life is short, Sam. You of all people know that. No one knows how long we have on this earth. We each of us have to grab at what happiness we can before it's too late. Your mother would've wanted me to be happy. She would want you to be happy too.'

Sam rubbed one of his hands over his face. 'Yeah, well, I'd like to be happy but you won't believe the mess I've made of things…'

His father listened as Sam told him what had happened. 'Sounds bad, son, especially when she won't even take your calls. What are going to do?'

'What are you doing for the next couple of days?' Sam asked. 'Do you fancy some time out on the boat?'

'Sure,' Jack said with a twinkle in his eyes. 'Are we going fishing?'

'Yeah,' Sam said with a slowly spreading smile. 'You could say that.'

Lexi was walking along the beach at Noosa on the Sunshine Coast of Queensland when she saw him. At first she thought she had imagined it, conjuring him up out of a bad case of wishful thinking. But the closer he came the faster her heart began to beat until it was even louder than the sound of the waves crashing against the shore.

She wanted to turn and walk back the other way. That's what her head was telling her to do but for some reason her feet weren't co-operating. They were stuck in the soft sand as if it had suddenly turned into concrete.

'Lexi,' Sam said, coming to stand in front of her.

She gave him a brittle look. 'I don't have anything to say to you.'

'Maybe not, but I have something to say to you.'

She rolled her eyes and started walking away. 'I can just imagine what it is,' she said, her bare feet making squeaking noises on the pristine sand. 'You want me to have a sordid little affair with you until you find someone else who interests you more.'

'No,' Sam said. 'That's not what I want to say. Anyway, no one interests me more than you do.'

'Sure, and I believe you,' Lexi said, throwing him a fulminating look over her shoulder.

Sam looked at her flushed features. Her long blond hair was blowing across her face and she kept flicking it back with angry movements of her hands. She looked like a mermaid. His very own gorgeous sea nymph. How could he have ever imagined his life without her in it? 'Don't you want to hear what I've come all this way to say?' he asked.

She frowned at him furiously. 'You think I would agree to have a relationship with you after the way you treated me?'

'You took me by surprise, turning up at the marina like that,' he said. 'I wasn't prepared. I needed more time to think things over.'

'*I* took you by surprise?' she flashed back. 'I thought you were going to welcome me with open arms and instead you sent me away as if I was nothing to you but an annoying little tramp.'

'I know,' Sam said. 'It was unforgiveable.'

'You've got *that* right, country boy,' she said, stomping away again.

Sam had to trot to keep up. He caught one of her arms and turned her round to face him. 'Lexi—'

'If you don't let me go this instant I'll scream for the lifeguard,' she said. 'I'll say you're attacking me. I'll tell him you're a stalker. I'll tell him you've been calling me about a hundred times and never saying anything, not a single word. I'll tell him…I'll tell him you broke my heart and I'll probably never ever be happy again…' She choked back a little sob.

Sam looked at her with melting eyes. 'Lexi, darling,' he said, holding her close so she couldn't run away again. 'You know how hopeless I am with words. I can only manage one or two when I'm feeling under pressure. I just clam up. But there are three words I wanted to say to your face. I love you.'

'No, you don't.' Her eyes flashed at him. 'I bet you're just saying that to get me back into your bed.'

Sam lifted her chin, a soft smile playing about

his mouth. 'I knew you probably wouldn't believe me so that's why I have a back-up plan.'

Lexi wrinkled her forehead. 'A…a what?'

Sam turned her so she was facing the ocean. There was a yacht out behind the small breakers. Lexi could just make out the name on the side—*Whispering Waves*. 'You sailed all the way up here?' she asked, looking back at him.

'Yeah,' he said. 'What do you say to a few days out there all by ourselves? You, me and the wind.'

Lexi pulled out of his hold. 'I think I'll pass,' she said stiffly, and continued walking.

'Darling, will you just give me a couple of minutes of your time?' he said. 'I have to get back to my yacht before my dad sails it into a reef or something.'

Lexi stopped and looked at him. 'Your dad's out there?'

'Yeah,' he said. 'One of us had to man the boat. I could hardly send him along the beach to ask you to marry me.'

She looked at him with her head at a wary angle. 'What did you say?'

Sam smiled at her. 'Will you marry me, Lexi?'

Lexi's eyes started to tear up. 'You want to marry me?' she asked in a choked-up voice

'Sure do,' he said. 'And I want everyone to know.' He turned her to face the sea. 'See?'

Lexi looked at the mainsail of Sam's yacht as the wind filled it, revealing the words in large blue letters: *Will you marry me, Lexi?*

'So what do you say, darling?' Sam asked. 'Will you be my wife and the mother of my babies? I don't care how many we have. I just know I want to have them with you.'

Lexi blinked back tears, her throat so tight with emotion she could barely speak. 'Yes,' she said, throwing herself into his arms. 'Yes!'

Sam swung her around, holding her tightly against his body. 'Thank heaven,' he said. 'You had me worried there for a moment.'

Lexi slipped down his body to look up at him. 'What changed your mind? I thought you never wanted to get married? I thought you didn't believe you could love someone enough to spend your whole life with them.'

He cupped her face in his hands. 'I watched my father grieve for my mother for twenty years. I swore I would never love someone that much.

But what I've realised is you can never love someone too much.' He pressed a gentle kiss to her mouth. 'You've taught me that, Lexi. Life is about loving with your whole being, not just part of yourself. And I want to spend the rest of my life loving you like that—totally, completely, absolutely.'

Lexi smiled as she looked into his soft dark brown eyes. 'How long do you think your father can handle that boat without you?' she asked.

'Not very long,' Sam said. 'Why?'

She looped her arms around his neck. 'Because I have something to see to first, that's why.'

'Oh?' he said. 'What's that?'

'This,' she said and pressed her mouth to his.

* * * * *

Mills & Boon® Large Print
Medical

December

SYDNEY HARBOUR HOSPITAL: BELLA'S WISHLIST	Emily Forbes
DOCTOR'S MILE-HIGH FLING	Tina Beckett
HERS FOR ONE NIGHT ONLY?	Carol Marinelli
UNLOCKING THE SURGEON'S HEART	Jessica Matthews
MARRIAGE MIRACLE IN SWALLOWBROOK	Abigail Gordon
CELEBRITY IN BRAXTON FALLS	Judy Campbell

January

SYDNEY HARBOUR HOSPITAL: MARCO'S TEMPTATION	Fiona McArthur
WAKING UP WITH HIS RUNAWAY BRIDE	Louisa George
THE LEGENDARY PLAYBOY SURGEON	Alison Roberts
FALLING FOR HER IMPOSSIBLE BOSS	Alison Roberts
LETTING GO WITH DR RODRIGUEZ	Fiona Lowe
DR TALL, DARK...AND DANGEROUS?	Lynne Marshall

February

SYDNEY HARBOUR HOSPITAL: AVA'S RE-AWAKENING	Carol Marinelli
HOW TO MEND A BROKEN HEART	Amy Andrews
FALLING FOR DR FEARLESS	Lucy Clark
THE NURSE HE SHOULDN'T NOTICE	Susan Carlisle
EVERY BOY'S DREAM DAD	Sue MacKay
RETURN OF THE REBEL SURGEON	Connie Cox